A CHASE FAMILY CHRISTMAS

LAUREN ROYAL

April 2020 Edition
CHASE FAMILY SERIES

A CHASE FAMILY CHRISTMAS by Lauren Royal

Published by Novelty Books, a division of Novelty Publishers, LLC, 205 Avenida Del Mar #275, San Clemente, CA 92674

ISBN: 978-1-63469-162-8

April 2020 Edition

Cover by Teresa Spreckelmeyer

Learn more about the author and her books at LaurenRoyal.com.

For all of my Jewel sisters

And especially for Cynthia Wright,
because becoming honorary sisters and friends
with the first romance author one ever read
is every romance writer's dream ccme true

CAST OF CHARACTERS

In order of appearance in this book…

Chrystabel, Lady Trentingham

Chrystabel appeared in *Never Doubt a Viscount*, *The Scandal of Lord Randal*, and *A Gentleman's Plot to Tie the Knot* as well as her own romance, *A Secret Christmas*. She is an irrepressible matchmaker.

Amethyst & Colin Chase
The Earl and Countess of Greystone

In *When an Earl Meets a Girl*, Amy, a jeweler's daughter and a jeweler herself, met Colin when he visited her family's shop. Amy & Colin have three children:

Jewel, age 21

Hugh, age 19
Aidan, age 15

Kendra Chase & Patrick Caldwell
The Duke and Duchess of Amberley
In *A Duke's Guide to Seducing His Bride*, Kendra and Trick
wed in a marriage arranged by her brothers. Kendra &
Trick have four children:
Elspeth, age 18
Diana, age 16
Castor, age 13
Pollux, age 13

Caithren & Jason Chase
The Marquess and Marchioness of Cainewood
In *How to Undress a Marquess*, Cait, a Scot who never
dreamed of wedding an Englishman, met Jason on the
road. Cait & Jason have three children:
Griffin, age 20
Adam, age 17
James, age 14

Violet & Ford Chase
The Viscount and Viscountess Lakefield

In *Never Doubt a Viscount,* Ford, an absentminded scientist, met Violet, an intellectual who never expected to wed, when he moved into the dilapidated house next door to her parents' splendid estate. Violet & Ford have three children:

Nicolas, age 15
Marcus, age 11
Rebecca, age 11

Rowan Ashcroft, the Viscount Tremayne

Rowan is Chrystabel's youngest child and Violet's brother. He was a childhood friend of Jewel's, but they have long since parted ways.

ONE

Saturday, November 20, 1688
Lakefield House, South of England

HE COUNTESS of Trentingham alighted from her carriage in front of the charming manor house, knowing her eldest daughter wasn't at home.

Chrystabel hadn't come to see Violet—rather, she wished to see her son-in-law, Ford Chase. Today was the perfect day, a day without distractions, as Violet had taken their three children to play with their young cousins at her sister Lily's house.

One of Chrystabel's primary joys was helping people find love, and, as usual, she had a plan.

"Hello, Harry," she said when Ford's elderly houseman answered the door. She pressed a bottle of perfume into his hands. "I've brought more Spiced Rosewater for your lovely wife."

"I thank you on Hilda's behalf, my lady. And mine as well."

"Is Lord Lakefield in his laboratory?"

"He is," Harry said. "Will you wait for him in the drawing room?"

"Oh, there's no need to make him come down. I'm happy to go up."

The houseman sniffed at the bottle and smiled as Chrystabel made her way past him and up two floors to the laboratory. The door was open, and Ford was inside, tinkering.

"Knock, knock," she called cheerfully.

Ford looked up, his gaze hazy as he shifted his attention to her. She watched his bright blue eyes clear. "Er, welcome."

"No need to feign enthusiasm." She knew he hated to be interrupted when he was in the middle of inventing something. "I won't take but a minute of your time."

He was holding a long, thin piece of metal, looking rather at a loss. "No, no, it's lovely to see you."

It was lovely of him to lie. "What are you working on there?"

"A new kind of skate. I hope. What brings you here today?"

"I shall get right to the point. You're hosting your family here for Christmas this year, are you not?"

He blinked. "I suppose so. Violet takes care of such things. But I reckon it's probably our turn."

Chrystabel knew it was their turn. The Chases alternated hosting the family Christmas celebration, progressing from oldest to youngest. His sister Kendra had hosted last year, which meant it was Ford's turn this year. Or rather, as he'd said, it was Violet's turn to act as hostess—because the last thing Chrystabel could imagine was her daughter's husband planning any sort of celebration.

If he did, he'd probably decorate with copper wire and botanical specimens in place of garlands and holly.

"Will your niece Jewel be here?" she asked.

"Of course. Everyone in the family attends. From the twenty-third until Christmas morning."

At which point he and Violet and their children would come to Trentingham Manor for the Ashcroft family Christmas. Chrystabel could scarcely wait to have all of her family together—her other daughters, Rose and Lily, their husbands, Kit and Rand, and all of her grandchildren. And her younger, unmarried son, twenty-three-year-old Rowan, who lived in London these days.

She loved Christmas. Maybe even more than she loved matchmaking.

"I have an idea for you," she said. "An idea to give Jewel a happy surprise."

He toyed with the thing in his hands. "Yes?"

"I'm thinking you might invite Rowan for Christmas Eve supper. He'll be coming for Christmas Day at Trentingham anyway, but he could arrive a day earlier to join you and Jewel for supper here."

His hands stopped fiddling with the strip of metal. He looked puzzled. "Jewel hasn't asked to see Rowan since she was a small child. I'm not sure she'd be interested."

"Of course she would! The two of them were the best of friends once upon a time."

He shrugged. "I'll ask Violet."

"Oh, but I was thinking you should also surprise Violet." Violet would put an end to this immediately, Chrystabel knew. But she also knew that Jewel and Rowan belonged together. These two young people would make a perfect match—and that match would be Chrystabel's crowning achievement. "Violet hasn't seen her brother in quite some time, now that he's living in London. Don't you think she'd enjoy the surprise, too?"

"I'm not sure…"

"Here," she said, pulling a sheet of parchment from her pocket. "I've written out a note for you, to make it easy for you to invite Rowan for Christmas Eve supper. All you need to do is copy it in your own hand and send it. I've written his direction on the back."

She held it out to him, leaving him no choice but to take it or appear rude.

"Very well," he said, setting it among the jumble of who-knows-what that sat on a table.

She wondered when he might next go through that jumble, searching for something he'd misplaced. Everything in his laboratory looked misplaced, at least to Chrystabel. Just her luck, he might not glance at that jumble again until after Christmas.

"Why don't you write the letter now?" she suggested. "In fact, I'll post it for you if you do." She pulled a clean sheet of paper from her pocket, unfolded it, and set it before him. "Christmas is naught but a month away, and Rowan could make other plans."

"Very well," he repeated, clearly anxious to get back to his work.

"This won't take but a moment." Spotting a few pens stuck in a beaker, Chrystabel snatched one up and handed it to him with an ink pot and a smile. "I'm so looking forward to Christmas."

TWO

Aᴍʏ

The next day
The kitchen in Greystone Castle

METHYST, THE Countess of Greystone (more commonly called Amy), was incredible at her jeweler's bench but incompetent in her kitchen. In consequence, she ventured into the massive stone chamber just one day each year, and today was that day.

As usual on this day, the last Sunday before the season of Advent, Amy found herself standing at the enormous wooden table in the center of the room, surrounded by bowls and spoons, cups and knives, an assortment of ingredients, and her family.

Well, most of her family, anyway.

Her youngest son, Aidan, had contrived to make himself scarce.

"I cannot believe William of Orange has finally invaded," nineteen-year-old Hugh announced with a touch of dangerous glee in his voice. "May I have some of that brandy to celebrate?"

"I suppose that's as good an excuse as any," his father agreed in a wry tone.

Amy smiled as she watched Colin pour their eldest son a small goblet of the amber spirits. With their emerald eyes and long, raven hair—Colin's now attractively touched with silver at the temples—the two looked so alike that she sometimes found herself looking at Hugh and daydreaming about years gone past.

After refreshing his own goblet, Colin set down the decanter. "I wouldn't call this an invasion, given that William's plans have been public knowledge since September."

"Well then, William has finally *landed*." Hugh sipped, looking as though he felt he were very grown up. "And I'm prepared to go off to war."

"Oh, no." Colin's goblet thudded to the scarred surface. "You're not going anywhere but Oxford. I will not allow my heir to risk his life."

"Your father is right." Amy's heart pounded at the mere thought of either of her sons engaged in battle. "And if you so much as mention this again, you won't even return to university. I will throw you in the oubliette until William and Mary are crowned."

Colin laughed. "There won't be any need for such measures. King James's support is dissolving already."

"As it should," Amy confirmed with a satisfied nod.

Her family wasn't alone in condemning the king for overturning the religion, laws, and liberties of his realm by suspending Parliament and consolidating power. Along with many others, the Chases had supported sending William of Orange an invitation that assured him the nobility and gentry were dissatisfied and would rally to his side. And since then, they'd been working behind the scenes in hopes of accomplishing a smooth transition without undue bloodshed.

She didn't, however, find this an uplifting subject for a day she looked forward to all year. Although she was glad to hear the 'invasion' was progressing with little loss of life, any chance of war, however slight, was unsettling.

"Can we discuss something else?" she asked, adding two splashes of milk to her big mixing bowl. "It's Stir-Up Sunday."

"Certainly," Hugh said flippantly, emboldened by the liquor. "Shall we discuss Stir-Up Sunday itself? If you ask me, that's a stupid name for a holy day."

His older sister, Jewel, looked up from the loaf of sugar she was grating. "Nobody asked you," she teased, flicking sugar at her brother.

"It isn't a holy day, Hugh." Amy added a portion of ground cinnamon to the bowl. "Merely the last Sunday in the Church Year. And the name comes from the opening words of this day's main prayer, which begins, 'Stir up, we beseech thee, O Lord—'"

"Balderdash!" Finished with the grating, Jewel licked sugar dust from her fingertips. "It's called Stir-Up Sunday because this is the day we all stir the Christmas plum pudding."

"Of course," Colin confirmed with a grin.

Enjoying their good-natured banter, Amy smiled to herself as she added the sugar. She consulted the splattered sheet of paper on the table. "Aunt Elizabeth says that next we add half a jack of good-quality brandy."

"This is *fine* brandy, which is much better than good-quality," Colin informed her, pouring another splash into his goblet.

Or maybe two or three splashes. Amy wasn't sure how much liquid comprised a proper splash. While Aunt Elizabeth had specified a number of splashes for various ingredients, she'd failed to define the size of one.

Amy could only hope she'd added the right amount of everything.

It wasn't easy making good plum pudding. She'd been tweaking this recipe for nearly twenty years, since she'd first found it tucked into a book in Greystone's ancient library. This year she'd asked

Aunt Elizabeth to give her advice on each ingredient's proportions, because the original recipe had listed only what went into the pudding, without any suggested measurements. The vast majority of receipt books failed to include that vital information.

Which was exactly why Amy usually kept out of the kitchen.

She preferred staying in her workshop, where everything made sense. Eighteen karat gold was eighteen parts gold to three parts copper and three parts silver—every jeweler knew that. In her workshop, she didn't have to puzzle over the size of a splash.

"Half a jack." Jewel cocked her head. "How big is a jack?"

"Eight big spoonfuls." Amy was grateful that Aunt Elizabeth had explained that, at least, in the notes she'd sent from France. "So we need four big spoonfuls of this brandy." She reached for the decanter.

"Not yet." Hugh snatched it up. "I want some more first."

"Hmm," Colin mused. "Perhaps I should fetch some *good*-quality brandy, so we can keep drinking this fine stuff."

"You were invited in here to stir," Amy protested. "Not to drink." Belying her words, she made some notations on the paper and let Hugh refill his goblet before she took the decanter. "Jewel, will you go see if Aidan has finished making the charms? Adding the brandy is the final step before the stirring."

She poured four spoonfuls of the brandy into the plum pudding mixture while Jewel went next door to the workshop.

At twenty-one, Amy's first-born was a lovely young lady. With her wavy dark hair and her father's emerald eyes, Jewel was pretty, pixieish, and full of life. She was also an accomplished stained-glass artist, which made her parents very proud.

What Jewel wasn't, though, was in love. For a while now, Amy had been wondering if her eldest would ever consent to wed anyone. While she adored her daughter's company and would never wish her away, she couldn't help hoping Jewel would head her own household someday—for Jewel's sake.

Just recently, however, Jewel had begun keeping company with a fine young viscount named Henry Breckenridge. Had Amy detected a new sparkle in her daughter's eyes, or was that only wishful thinking? By this time next year, she thought, Jewel might be wed and on her way to motherhood.

Her fingers were secretly crossed.

Amy's middle child had gone off to Oxford at seventeen, exactly on schedule, as befitted an earl in the making. At nineteen, Hugh was learning how to manage the earldom during the weeks between terms. Though she hoped many more years would pass before

Hugh needed to take over, Amy had no doubt he would excel at following in his father's footsteps.

But her youngest, Aidan, worried her.

Jewel returned with fifteen-year-old Aidan in tow. "Yes, yes, I finished the charms," he grumbled. "Here."

Walking closer, he opened his hand. The silver charms tumbled onto the table, knocking into the silver penny Amy had already set there. A tiny ring, a tiny thimble, a tiny wishbone, and a tiny anchor.

"They're beautiful!" she exclaimed enthusiastically. "Exquisite little works of art! We will surely have the most lovely pudding tokens in all of England."

Aidan just grunted, which wasn't unexpected. But it was troubling.

It made Amy's heart drop to her knees and her mind go spinning back in time.

Much had happened in her forty-four years, but a few memories remained as clear and vivid as the day they were formed, seared onto her very soul. One of them was the last conversation she ever had with her beloved father.

"Promise me, Amy," he'd said just a day before he'd perished in the Great Fire of London. *"You have a gift that cannot be wasted, an obligation in your blood. Promise me that Goldsmith & Sons won't end with you."*

She hadn't wanted to wed the man he'd chosen for her, hadn't wanted to make this promise. But he'd worn her down.

She'd had no choice. No escape from the path that defined her life, the road her ancestors had put her on.

"You have my promise."

"I love you, poppet."

"I love you too, Papa."

As of yet, Goldsmith & Sons, her family's centuries-old jewelry concern, *had* ended with her—and every fond remembrance of her Papa was tinged with guilt, knowing she had defied his wishes. But Aidan was destined to reestablish the business, to set her world to rights.

She continued stirring the brandy into her mixture with a little more vigor than was necessary. "You're going to make such a marvelous jeweler."

"I don't want to be a jeweler," Aidan forced through gritted teeth. His unusual eyes—amethyst, like Amy's own—narrowed as he focused on her. "You should know that by now; I've certainly told you enough times."

Years before he was born—before any of their children were born, in fact—Colin had promised Amy that their second son would fulfill her pledge to her father. It was the greatest gift Colin had ever given her, and she'd been waiting twenty-one years for that promise to come to fruition.

But her second son wasn't cooperating.

And neither was his father.

In twenty-two years of marriage, Amy couldn't

remember ever having been quite this aggravated with Colin.

Aidan had turned fifteen half a year ago, at which point he should have been apprenticed to a jeweler to learn the trade—to acquire the skills he'd need to run a shop—in preparation for assuming his role. But he didn't want to do that. And Colin was on his side.

"Our son should be able to go his own way," Colin said now, for at least the tenth time. "Leave him alone."

Trying her best to appear patient, Amy turned to her youngest for at least the tenth time as well. She decided to take a new tack. "What will you do instead?" she asked as reasonably as she could manage. "You're a second son—you won't inherit. Will you take up soldiering or preaching?"

Aidan's jaw remained set. "I don't know what I want to do. I only know what I *don't* want to do."

Amy released a gusty sigh. "Of all the stubborn, foolish—"

"Amy." Colin sidled up to her and gently removed the spoon from her hand, his expression equal parts sympathy and strain. "Come with me," he coaxed, drawing her out into the corridor.

Once there, he moved close. Very close. Amy inhaled his spicy scent, and her senses began to spin in an entirely too familiar way.

"Can we let this go?" he asked. "It's Stir-Up Sunday. One of your favorite days of the year." Leaning closer still, he pressed a soft kiss to Amy's lips—a soft kiss that turned into more, no matter that their offspring doubtless knew exactly what they were doing in the corridor outside the kitchen.

Amy's heart raced, same as ever—Colin knew how to calm her down. Or maybe he knew how to stir her up, which was fitting for Stir-Up Sunday. Fitting and thrilling and annoying, all at the same time. But mostly thrilling, she couldn't help thinking. Twenty-two years married, and her husband could still make her blood sing through her veins. In the thrall of such bliss, she had a hard time staying miffed with him.

Except for the small part of her that held back, the tiny voice that whispered in her head, reminding her he wasn't taking her side.

It was easy to ignore that voice now, kissed and loved in Colin's arms. Over the past few months, she'd become accustomed to ignoring it.

But it never quite went away.

"Very well," she said, a mite breathless as she broke the kiss. "Let's go back in and stir."

When the two of them reentered the room, Jewel, Hugh, and Aidan all rolled their eyes—a habit they had picked up from their father. "It's time to stir," Colin said firmly.

Traditionally, every child gave the mixture a stir and made a wish while doing so. But Amy had changed the longstanding tradition years ago, to include everyone in her family, not just the children—who weren't really children anymore, she realized with a little tug of her heart.

Her first Christmas as a Chase had been her first experience with tokens in the plum pudding as well—at that point, only a coin, a ring, and a thimble. But as Amy and Colin had Jewel and then Hugh and then Aidan, she had added more charms over the years, so each member of their family could stir and make a wish.

Aidan's tokens were truly beautiful, more detailed every year. That told her his heart was in goldsmithing, even if his head hadn't caught up yet. But she wouldn't push him again today. "Aidan?" she asked.

They always went from youngest to oldest.

Aidan's soft smile reassured his mother that for now he was putting their disagreement behind him. Her heart sang with joy. "I choose the coin," he said, picking the only charm he hadn't made himself.

"A fortune in the offing," Amy murmured, wondering if her youngest was hoping some unexpected fortune might save him from his destiny. But that was silly, because the meanings were for the lucky people who found the charms in their portion on Christmas Eve, not for whoever stirred them into the pudding. "Make a wish," she reminded him, handing him the long wooden spoon. "And stir from east to west, to honor the Magi and their journey in that direction."

As he dropped the coin into the batter, Aidan closed his eyes. "I wish..." he whispered, stirring the mixture fiercely.

Amy feared he wished he wouldn't have to become a jeweler's apprentice. But she kept that to herself and turned to her other son. "Hugh?"

Hugh chose the anchor, which symbolized safe harbor. "I wish..."

Amy had no idea what he was wishing. But she hoped it was for a long and fruitful life. And *not* for a chance to go off to war. "Jewel?"

"I choose the wishbone," Jewel declared. "For good luck for all of us!"

Amy had been hoping Jewel would choose the ring, a sign of marriage. So she chose the ring for herself, wishing her only daughter would soon find the love of her life.

"Colin?"

"All that's left is the thimble," he complained. "What on earth does that signify again?"

"A life of blessedness," Amy reminded him.

And as he stirred the thimble into the plum pudding, she couldn't help thinking they indeed lived a life of blessedness. Whatever troubles they had, they were blessed.

All five of them.

THREE

Kendra

A month later
Very early Friday, December 23
Amberley House

 T TWO HOURS past midnight, the Duchess
of Amberley was wrapping the last of her gifts
when she finally gave up hoping the duke would arrive
home in time for Christmas.

Kendra tied the final ribbon with a sigh. In twenty
years of marriage, she and her husband—Patrick,
though she called him Trick—had never spent her
favorite holiday apart. But Trick had been summoned to
Scotland, where his father was dying, and Kendra

hadn't been able to go with him, because the twins were ill and she had been loath to leave them.

More than two months later, all four of their children were healthy, but Trick still hadn't returned.

Oh, he'd sent messages. One after another, full of excellent excuses. His father lived longer than expected— that had been a good thing, giving the two of them precious extra time together. When Hamish finally passed on, the wake lasted a week. After that, Trick's brother Niall had needed his help to settle their father's affairs, and then a big storm hit, keeping him from leaving.

Nine long weeks. Kendra missed Trick's smile. She missed his companionship. She missed his quick wit.

But most of all, she missed Trick in her bed.

God, did she miss Trick in her bed.

"Your grace? Are you all right?"

"Oh!" Kendra whirled to see her lady's maid in the doorway. "You scared me. Goodness, Margaret, we're leaving for Lakefield first thing in the morning. What are you doing up at this hour?"

"Waiting for you to go to bed, your grace," the young woman said through a yawn. "Pray pardon. I'm not as sleepy as I appear."

"Of course you're sleepy." The poor girl looked exhausted, her russet hair drooping along with her shoulders. "There's no need for you to wait up for me. I *can* undress myself, you know."

"I don't want you to have to undress yourself. I owe you and your husband everything, your grace."

Margaret had grown up at Trick's orphanage. Kendra liked to hire the orphans when they came of age, to make sure they were trained properly before finding them other employment. "You owe us nothing, Margaret. You've done us proud. In fact, you've grown into such a fine lady's maid that I think it's time for us to find you a permanent position."

A wave of panic filled the maid's big blue eyes. "A permanent position, your grace? With whom? Where?"

"With a fine lady anywhere. London, perhaps. Wouldn't that be exciting?"

"No! Can I not stay here at Amberley? I'll do anything, your grace. I'll wash laundry. I'll scrub floors. Anything at all. I'll go back to the orphanage—"

"My heavens, Margaret, there's no need to get over-wrought. You're too old for the orphanage." Thinking about Trick's orphanage made Kendra think about Trick, which made her restless. "We'll discuss this another time. Go on to bed."

"If you're sure you have no need of assistance, your grace."

"I'm sure." Kendra didn't want help tonight. She wanted to be alone with her disappointment. "Good night."

Tying a ribbon around the last gift, Kendra listened

as Margaret's footsteps faded into the distance. Then she placed the gift on the pile with all the others and left the sitting room.

She'd been having trouble falling asleep these past weeks in her lonely, lonely bed. But it was very late, and she'd spent the day busily preparing for travel, so she had high hopes of dropping off quickly. To ensure that, she took a detour to the pantry to collect a decanter of wine.

Then nearly spilled it when she reached her chamber to find Trick there, sitting on the large wooden chest at the foot of their bed, pulling off his boots.

"What—when did you arrive?" she gasped, rushing over to throw her arms around him.

He laughed. "Only just now. I've been riding all day. Thought I'd find you in here so late at night, but I didn't. Wanted to get these muddy boots off before I went looking for you—"

His explanation was cut off when Kendra pressed her mouth to his.

The kiss was demanding, intoxicating, wild with long-denied desire. She felt herself sinking into it, savoring the velvet warmth she'd so missed.

Before she was ready, Trick broke it off. "Um, *leannan*? I think you're spilling something down my back."

"Oh, my God." She stepped away, righting the

decanter she'd tipped. "It's wine," she said, walking over to set it on the dressing table. "I'm sorry. Let's get this wine-wet shirt off of you."

He rose, and his fingers went to the laces at his throat. "Is that a gleam I see in your eye, *leannan*?"

"I've missed you." She went on her toes to pull the shirt off over his head. "I want you," she added, running her hands down his bare chest. "Oh, you're cold."

"Sixteen hours on the road in winter will chill the bones a bit. And I want you, too—so much—but I haven't had a proper bath since I left Scotland."

"Well, let's ring for one, then. Quickly."

"Already done. In fact, I believe it's arriving now." He sat back down on the chest. "I wouldn't mind some of that wine while we wait."

Kendra pulled two goblets from a cabinet and filled them while three burly footmen brought the big wooden tub inside and placed it in a corner. She handed Trick one of the goblets. More sleepy servants paraded in with steaming buckets of water.

Meanwhile, she fetched soap and some towels, anxious for everyone to leave so she could be alone with Trick again. Remembering him climbing into a tub with her more than once, she thought she'd do the same. She would wash him.

She couldn't wait to get her hands on him.

She couldn't believe he was here. After weeks apart, he was here. Her whole body seemed on fire.

"Quickly," she told the servants. "Quickly."

At last, she and Trick were alone. As the door closed behind the last footman, Trick pushed his breeches down and off and stepped into the tub.

Hurrying into their dressing room, Kendra kicked off her shoes, suddenly wishing she had Margaret to help her. Stockings, stomacher, laces, overdress, underskirt...undressing seemed to take forever, even though she didn't bother to put anything away, opting to leave it all on the floor for Margaret or someone else to pick up in the morning.

At long last she walked back to the bedroom, approaching her husband with a big smile. And stopped short.

"Trick?"

His head was tilted back against the edge of the tub, his empty goblet on the floor beside it. He looked to be sound asleep.

"Trick?" She walked over and jogged his shoulder. "Trick, wake up so we can get you washed and into bed."

Not a sound. Not a movement. Nothing.

"Trick?" She shook him harder.

"Tired," he murmured. A moment later he was snoring.

He was home, and she was burning. Moreover, she was standing beside him, naked as the day she was born —and he was sleeping. "Curses," she said aloud and knelt down to wash him.

He slept on.

FOUR

CAITHREN

Later that morning
Cainewood Castle

HE MARCHIONESS of Cainewood was finding her bodice unusually tight. Had she been eating too much of late? Caithren frowned down at the strained fabric as her maid loosened the lacing a wee bit and tied a firm bow.

"I'd like to discuss something before we leave," her husband said.

"Oh, aye?" It sounded important. "I can finish here, Ida," she told her maid. "Please make sure my trunks made it onto one of the baggage carts."

As the young woman left, Jason dismissed his valet as well.

"Do I look plump in this gown?" Cait asked when the two of them were alone.

Jason was busy pulling on his boots. "Of course not," he said. "You look lovely."

It took everything Cait had not to snort. "Don't look up. What color is my gown?"

"Blue?" he guessed.

"Green. Christmas green. You can look up now."

He did. And grinned. "You do look lovely. Since Ida left, would you like some help with that stomacher?"

"After twenty-one years in England, I reckon I've mastered English clothes. But you can help if it makes you happy."

"It does." He rose and stood behind her, reaching around her to fasten the tabs. "Twenty-one years," he echoed, his breath warm by her cheek. "Unbelievable, isn't it?"

She nodded. "It's gone so fast. I don't feel any older, but the lads are all but grown." Griffin was twenty, Adam seventeen, and their youngest, James, had turned fourteen over the summer.

Cait remembered the day James was born like yesterday: the entire family cramming into her bedchamber to meet him, Kendra bringing a gift of Leslie tartan to wrap him in. Cait still had that precious blanket, and she couldn't help sniffing it once in a while, imagining she could smell Jamie's sweet newborn scent. Someday she would wrap a grandchild in that tartan. Considering how quickly the years were speeding by, she feared that day could come alarmingly soon.

"What did you want to talk about?" she asked.

Thankfully the stomacher hid the fact that her bodice was too tight. Jason turned her to face him and gave her a light kiss. "Twenty-one years," he murmured again against her lips, "and nearly twenty years since we've gone anywhere alone together." He pulled back. "As we've readied for this short journey, I've been aware of how much trouble it always is to travel with all five of us. How many carriages we need, how many servants, how much baggage. Wouldn't it be pleasant to go somewhere on our own? Next summer, perhaps, we could visit your cousin in Scotland."

"And leave the lads behind? We've never left the lads."

"My point exactly, sweet. Don't you think it's about time? Jamie will be fifteen by then, and Griffin will have graduated from Oxford. We could leave Griffin here to play marquess for a few weeks, and take Adam and Jamie to stay at Greystone."

Caithren tilted her head to one side, considering. "I daresay Griffin could manage on his own for a bit…"

"Indeed, and therefore *we* could be on *our* own. Alone, Cait, just the two of us…doesn't that sound delightful? Remember our courtship on the road?"

She couldn't help but burst out laughing. "Oh, aye. I remember being at each other's throats much of the time."

He grinned, then cupped her face and brushed a thumb across her cheek. "Our first journey to Scotland wasn't like that," he reminded her in a low, meaningful tone.

Something fluttered in her stomach. "Aye, that journey was wonderful," she agreed, remembering their last holiday without bairns.

All in all, it had been marvelous. The one black mark on the lovely memory was that she'd decided to keep her first pregnancy from him, for fear he might cancel their plans. He hadn't been happy about that. But she and the babe had been fine, and she'd promised to never hide news like that again, and he'd forgiven her.

As fast as the years had sped by, it seemed forever since she and Jason had gone anywhere without all the complications that went with three offspring, as he'd said. It seemed a lifetime since they'd traveled that carefree, since they'd done anything just to please themselves—and each other.

"Very well," she finally said. "I suppose the lads are old enough to spend a month or so without us next summer."

"Excellent! I cannot wait. You'll see, Cait, this will be a brand-new chapter for us." He caught her up in another kiss—a kiss that made her wish they didn't have to leave so soon for his brother's house.

Or wait till next summer to journey alone together.

When he finally pulled away, he eyed her cleavage displayed in the tight gown. "Hmm..." he murmured, bending to kiss her there, too. "You're as slim as ever, and you know it—not plump in the least—but I will say *these* look pleasingly plump in this gown. Is it new?"

She laughed again. He never noticed her clothes, which meant she could order any that she wanted. "Yes, it's new for the holidays. Perhaps Mrs. Bletchley wrote down the wrong measurements." She frowned down at herself—her smallish breasts *did* look exceedingly plump framed in the neckline. "The rest of my new gowns are already packed. Perhaps I should wear an old one that fits me better."

"Don't be daft. I said you look lovely, and I meant it."

"Very well, I'll wear it, but mostly to avoid delaying our departure. I'm so looking forward to Christmas—I can already taste the plum pudding."

"You can?" he asked, turning away to grab his surcoat. "I thought you didn't like plum pudding." He swiveled back, alarm on his face. "Bloody hell, you're not with child, are you? What a calamity that would be!"

"Crivvens, of course not!" Her heart pounded at the mere thought. "I'm forty-three! Jamie's fourteen years old! Why would you say such a thing?" She glanced down again at her *pleasingly plump* breasts. If Mrs. Bletchley had measured correctly, she must have gained weight in the meantime. "By all the saints, I must stop eating so much!"

"You're not eating too much. But I've never seen you eat plum pudding—except the three Christmases you were with child."

They both stayed silent while Cait's mind raced. She usually did choose another sweet in place of plum pudding—he'd been right to say she hadn't ever really liked it. How much time had passed since her last monthly course? She couldn't think straight enough to recall. But swelling breasts...

And plum pudding...

Perhaps reacting to the look of horror she suspected was on her face, Jason broke the tension with a chuckle. "I was jesting, love," he said. "After all these years, of course you're not with child. Why should that happen now?"

She swallowed hard. "Maybe because we often do the thing that makes children happen?"

"Fourteen years, Cait. No children and no miscarriages. I think God has sent a clear message that our family is complete. Eat all the plum pudding you want. Now that you've learned how to master English clothes, it's about time you learned to enjoy English food."

Maybe he was right, she thought, her heart calming

a little. Maybe she craved plum pudding because she was finally learning to enjoy English food, and maybe that's why she'd gained weight, too. Or maybe the blasted dress was just too tight—maybe Mrs. Bletchley had mismeasured.

She couldn't be with child.

Could she?

FIVE

Amberley House

ENDRA WOKE late that morning. And she didn't wake on her own—she woke to someone gently rubbing her back.

She rolled languidly over, thrilled to find Trick in bed next to her, gazing at her with his heart in his amber eyes. She hadn't dreamed that he'd actually come home, then. He really was here.

She gave him a soft smile. "You're up," she said huskily, sleepiness in her voice.

"Awake, if not up." His voice was clear; evidently he'd wakened well before her. Watching her closely, adoringly, he pushed her hair off her face.

His fingers felt smooth and warm. The gesture made Kendra feel like the breathless innocent she'd been when she first met him.

"I cannot believe I fell asleep before we made love last night," he said with a heartfelt sigh. "This last week on the road, all I could think of was getting home so I could have you in my arms. And then..."

"You can have me in your arms now." Still sleepy, Kendra moved closer to hold him near, intertwining her legs with his. He felt heavenly. "Have you any memory of how difficult it was for me to get you clean and dry and into bed last night? You were like a rag doll—like one of Elspeth's or Diana's old rag dolls. Except much heavier."

"I remember trying to be as cooperative as I could, which I gather wasn't much." He chuckled before he kissed her—a quick kiss, yet hot enough to make her head reel. Hot enough to bring her wide awake. It had been so long since they'd been together this way. Entirely too long. "It seems several sixteen-hour days on the road took their toll," he added mournfully.

"Well, thank heavens you're here now. All clean and toasty warm, and I am so ready—"

He cut her off with another kiss, a kiss full of weeks of pent-up desire. His arms tightened around her as he explored her mouth as though tasting her for the first time, rather than after twenty years of marriage.

Kendra's heart raced as she pressed against him, anxious for more.

He wasn't wearing anything beneath the coverlet— he never did wear anything to sleep, and she wouldn't have been able to wrestle any nightclothes onto him in any case, after that frustrating bath. But she had donned a nightgown before joining him in their bed, and he reached for the hem now.

She pulled up on the garment, trying to help. She couldn't wait to get out of it, to feel him skin to skin. But as he yanked it off over her head, a knock came at the door.

Kendra grabbed the nightgown from his hands and stuffed it under the covers.

Trick stifled a laugh. Or maybe it was a groan. "Yes?" he called.

"Your grace?" His valet opened the door, and Kendra clutched the coverlet to her chin as three footmen followed him in. "I've learned you're leaving for Lakefield this morning, your grace, and I'm not to go with you." Edmund had traveled to Scotland with Trick and apparently been unaware of today's Christmas plans. "Her grace's belongings and all of your children's are already on the baggage cart. We must pack your things immediately."

"*Now*, Edmund?" It was more a growl than a question.

Edmund looked taken aback. "Shall we give you a few minutes to rise?"

"At the least."

The four men beat a hasty retreat.

No sooner had the door closed behind them than Trick reached for Kendra.

"Not now," she whispered in horror, scooting away.

"Why not? I sent them away. Come here, *leannan*."

"They'll come back any minute."

"No, they won't."

"How do you know? A few minutes, Edmund said."

"I know because I'm the duke, and a duke's valet doesn't interrupt the duke when he's asked to be left alone. Besides, we can be quick."

"I don't want to be quick." Yearning for much more, she released a resigned sigh. "Let's get up and go down to breakfast."

"I don't want to go down to breakfast." He was running his hands all over her, making her pulse pound, making her senses spin, making her weaken. Every inch of her felt sensitive, felt alive, felt amazing.

He leaned closer to capture her lips with his.

"No." She pulled away, a supreme effort. "Let's get dressed and find another place to do this, then."

"I'm not getting dressed when all I want is to be *undressed*. Too many damned layers." With a gigantic sigh she suspected was mostly for show, he rolled away and out of bed. "I'll fetch two robes and we'll find another room."

When he returned from the dressing room, Kendra rose on shaky legs. She shrugged into the robe he handed her. Burning for him, she stood still while he tied the sash around her waist as one might for a small child. It took all she had not to grab him close and fall back onto the bed.

"Let's go," he husked out, clearly just as inflamed as she was.

She loved the wild look in his beautiful amber eyes. But she wanted those eyes closed. She wanted him kissing her. "Where?"

"Another bedchamber. God knows the last duke designed plenty of extra bedchambers into this damned mansion."

"What will the servants think when they find a rumpled bed in a room that hasn't been used for months?"

"Why should you care what they think? You're the duchess. They're servants. We pay them not to think."

"For heaven's sake, Trick, will you fault me for having some decency? Let's go to the library. We can use one of the couches there. We won't have to rumple a bed."

"Very well. Let's go, then." He pulled her out of the room.

She laughed as he raced down the corridor, dragging

her by the hand behind him, both of them barefoot. She was forty-three years old and felt fourteen. This was ridiculous.

But when he pulled her into the library and slammed the door closed behind them, she didn't feel ridiculous. She felt desperate.

The library was huge and deep, a long room with furniture scattered all around and a lofty, fancy gilded ceiling. They dashed inside and fell to the nearest high-backed red leather couch, which faced away from the door. Trick deftly untied her sash while she fumbled with his, the two of them kissing frantically all the while.

Before opening, the door rattled—luckily—and they bolted to sit upright, hastily closing their robes.

Their eldest daughter, Elspeth, walked in and past the couch, then turned, looking surprised to find them there. "Da, you're home! We missed you!" She ran to Trick, bending down to give him a hug.

"I missed you, too," Trick said.

"What are you two doing in here?"

"Just having a discussion," Kendra said, hoping she didn't sound as breathless as she felt. "What are *you* doing in here?"

"I thought I'd find a book to take to Lakefield House." Elspeth was tall and golden-haired, with amber eyes like Trick's—it was fitting that they'd named her after his mother. "I don't want to interrupt you, though. Shall I come back later?"

Her lovely, full-sleeved pink gown made Kendra feel conspicuously naked. "No, no," she said. "Choose your book now."

Trick elbowed her in the ribs.

Elspeth walked to the far end of the library, where she took a good ten minutes to choose a book—ten minutes during which Trick and Kendra exchanged inanities while he slipped a hand inside her robe to tease her. He'd always been skilled at teasing her and hadn't unlearned anything during his long absence.

Kendra was burning. She was dying. She was wishing her dear daughter away.

Was she really wishing her daughter away? She loved her children beyond measure. But right now, right this moment—

Trick snatched his hand back when Elspeth approached, book in hand.

"Breakfast was being laid out when I came up here," she told her parents.

"We'll be down in a minute." That was Trick, because Kendra found herself incapable of saying anything.

"Very well, then, I'll see you downstairs." Slanting a final curious glance at her barefoot mother and father, Elspeth left the room.

"Lock the door," Kendra demanded breathlessly.

Trick rose and went over to close the door. Kendra heard a groan. "There's no lock. How is it that all these years I've never noticed there's no lock?"

"This is a library, not a bedchamber. We've never had any reason to lock the door before."

"Why on earth isn't that lass married by now?" Back beside Kendra, Trick was ripping open his robe. "She's eighteen already. She shouldn't be here."

"I was twenty-three when we wed." Kendra untied her own sash this time, reclining back on the couch and beckoning him closer. "You're not really wishing her away, are you? Just because she wanted a book?"

Evidently deciding that question didn't deserve an answer, Trick came over her and crushed his mouth to hers. He crushed his body to hers, too. Kendra wrapped her arms around him in an effort to pull him even closer. She twined her fingers in the hair on the nape of his neck and kissed him back with all the passion she'd been saving up the past two months. His hands went everywhere, stroking her into a frenzy.

Just as he inserted a knee between hers, the door opened again. Again! They bolted upright and clothed themselves once more.

"Da!" their daughter Diana cried, running in. "Elspeth said you're home!"

"That I am, sweetheart," Trick said, reaching to return her hug.

Kendra said nothing. She didn't have any words in her.

"I'm so glad to see you, Da." Diana's green eyes sparkled, matching her ruffled emerald dress. She was petite with dark red hair like Kendra's. Still mute, Kendra was trying not to wish her away. "What time will we be leaving for Lakefield?"

"Straight after breakfast."

"Oh, good. Breakfast is starting now."

"We'll be down in a minute. Close the door on your way out, will you?"

Trick waited until Diana left before daring to meet Kendra's eyes. "I suppose I cannot wish this one away, either?"

"She's only sixteen. You cannot wish her married at sixteen."

"And I wouldn't wish her away anyway," he said with an exaggerated sigh.

"Of course you wouldn't. What kind of parent would that make you?" Kendra launched herself at him.

"Ooof!" He laughed, and then their mouths were sealed together and they were fighting with their sashes again.

Some time passed. Three or four minutes? Ten? Kendra wasn't sure—all she knew was a haze of long-denied passion. All she knew was her dear husband's mouth and his hands and his body—

Until the thirteen-year-old twins walked in, forcing the two of them to bolt upright yet again.

"Diana told us you were in here," Castor said. "Why aren't you at breakfast?

"We're all waiting," Pollux added.

The boys were identical, with golden hair like Trick's and eyes greener than Kendra's. Thanks to their mother's love of mythology, Castor, Pollux, and Diana all bore names of Roman gods. But the twins preferred to be called Cas and Pol. "Pronounced like Paul the Apostle," Pollux informed anyone who would listen.

Trick had once confided that he understood his son's feelings. Having been called an unusual name all his life, he sympathized with Pol's desire for a more normal one.

"I'm so glad to see you're both feeling better," he said now, since the twins' illness in October had kept the family from accompanying him to Scotland.

"But we're missing breakfast!" Cas said again. "Won't you come down to the dining room? We can't leave for Christmas till we've eaten."

"We'll be down in a minute," Trick said for the third time. "Run along."

The twins left the door open. Which was just as well.

"I suppose we'd best go down to breakfast," Kendra said with a heartfelt sigh.

Trick's sigh was even more elaborate. "Bloody hell, I suppose you're right."

SIX

COLIN

On the road to Lakefield House

N ALL OF his years, Colin Chase couldn't remember a Christmas as vexing as this one.

While his parents were away during the Civil War, his childhood Christmases had been celebrated with naught but his siblings and a few servants. Those had been rather quiet, yet still enjoyable. He'd spent most of his young adult life at King Charles II's court, in exile on the Continent—while those Christmases had been filled with false gaiety, he recalled them as pleasant nonetheless. And the many Christmases since he'd wed Amy...all of those he remembered as blissful (whether they'd actually been blissful or not).

But *this* Christmas, his daughter, Jewel, who was usually so high-spirited, had quite suddenly become withdrawn. He wished he could figure out why.

Worse, his older son, Hugh, was all too eager to go off to war. Which he didn't need to figure out—he suspected he might have felt the same at Hugh's age, after all—but he did need to thwart.

Even worse, his younger son, Aidan, was rebelling. Which Colin figured was his main problem.

Because, worst of all, thanks to Aidan, he and Amy weren't seeing eye to eye.

Which was absolutely miserable.

It seemed to him that the whole family's mood had been steadily deteriorating in the weeks since Stir-Up Sunday. *Vexing* did not even begin to describe the tension in their carriage as they made their way to his younger brother's house for what was supposed to be a festive holiday.

He decided to break the sullen silence by tackling the simplest issue first. In fact, he thought with an unexpected flash of insight, he actually might know the reason Jewel's state of mind had plummeted yesterday.

"Your new blue gown is lovely," he told her from across the carriage's cabin, secretly thinking it matched her all-too-blue disposition. "But you seem pensive. I'm very sorry you lost your maid." Lydia had been with Jewel since childhood, transitioning from nursemaid to lady's maid. "As soon as we get back, we'll find you another one."

"I care not that Lydia left," Jewel said. When she saw his look of surprise, she added, "That is, of course I care, but I understand that she must look after her mother now."

"Then why are you brooding?"

Jewel's glare made it clear that had been the wrong thing to say.

"I'm sorry," he recanted and tried again. "Why have you been so quiet?"

"Leave her alone," Amy said. "Girls brood some times of the month."

Jewel let out an indignant huff. "Very well," she snapped, "it's Lydia. Gads."

It was dim inside the carriage, but not so dim that Colin couldn't tell Jewel had turned red. Which was no wonder, given her mother's insensitive comment. Amy wasn't usually so short-tempered. She must be even more upset with him than he'd thought.

Bloody hell.

"Are we there yet?" Aidan asked.

"Does it *look* like we're there?" Sitting between her two brothers, Jewel gestured out the carriage window, somehow managing to continue looking peeved yet also grateful to be on another subject. "Snowy fields and more fields. Snowy hills. Do you see a river, dear brother? Lakefield is on the Thames."

"Patience," Colin counseled his youngest. "We've been on the road less than an hour."

"Patience isn't his strong point," Hugh said.

Aidan leaned across his sister to scowl at his older brother.

"Aidan is patient at a jeweler's bench," their mother disagreed. "Endlessly patient, getting every detail right. Which is why he will do a wonderful job of bringing Goldsmith & Sons back to life."

"I'm a Chase!" Aidan exploded. "I'm not a Goldsmith, so there will be no Goldsmith & Sons! Let me out of here!" He banged on the ceiling of the carriage, and it ground to a halt.

The moment it stopped, he threw open the door and jumped out.

"Aidan!" Amy started after him.

"Sit." His hand on her shoulder, Colin stuck his head out the door to have a look, then ducked back inside. "The coachman made room for him up front. He's wearing a heavy cloak. He'll be fine. Let him ride there and calm down." He reseated himself beside her as the carriage began moving again. "Why do you have to keep pushing him?"

"Because it's important to me. Because you promised."

It had been a mistake to make that promise, Colin knew now. A mistake to promise another man's life away, even if that other man was his as-yet-unconceived son. But a Chase promise was not given lightly—nor was it ever broken.

He sighed. "We've been talking about this for months now. Can you let it go for Christmas? Just for Christmas?"

For a good long while, Amy just looked at him. Then to their two older children and back to him.

"Very well," she said at last. "But only for Christmas."

Which gave him a few days' reprieve to figure out how to fix this. "Thank you," he said and kissed her on the forehead.

Her soft smile tamed his vexation a bit. It wasn't the first time they'd disagreed in all their years together, and he was certain it wouldn't be the last. But somehow, some way, for both their sakes and for Aidan, he would find a way to make this right.

SEVEN

KENDRA

Lakefield House

*T*HANKS TO their much-delayed breakfast, Kendra's family was the last to arrive at Lakefield House.

While her children spilled out of the carriage and ran inside, she lingered a moment to look around. A smile spread on her face as she took in the garlands of ivy draping the stone walls. A large red bow hung over the main door and each window, the swagged ends wound with holly and laurel.

"Violet did a wonderful job," she said as Trick stepped out beside her. "I love Christmas."

"I love *you*," he whispered in her ear, "and I cannot wait to find out which bedroom we're assigned."

She laughed as they followed the girls and the twins inside.

Indoors, the honey-toned paneled entry hall was also asplash with red and green. At its end, where it opened up to the drawing room, Kendra paused to enjoy the splendor.

Once called the great hall, the soft-turquoise-hued chamber was vast enough to hold a harpsichord and several groupings of comfortable furniture. Winter foliage twined with red ribbon lined the mantel of the massive fireplace. Beeswax candles sat on the windowsills, waiting to be lit when darkness fell. Cloth of gold was swagged lavishly up the staircase, held in place at intervals with big red bows.

Her brothers were all gathered there with their wives. "The duchess arrives at last," Colin called out drolly. "What took you so long?"

Thinking about what took her so long, Kendra felt herself turning red. Trick laughed and seized the opportunity to kiss her, reaching overhead to pull a berry off the kissing bush that hung over the room's entrance. Made of two wooden hoops arranged to make a sphere, it was decked with evergreen, ribbons, and rosy little apples, all surrounding a spring of mistletoe that dangled in its center.

"How long have you been married, dear twin?" her

brother Ford teased. "So long that your husband needs mistletoe as an excuse to kiss you?"

"Twenty years," she shot back. "And we don't need mistletoe—"

Her words were cut off when she sneezed.

And sneezed again.

"What on earth is going on here?" she asked, pulling a handkerchief from her sleeve and holding it to her nose. Pressing hard on her upper lip, she barely managed to stop a third sneeze. "You don't have a *cat* in here, do you?" She looked to Violet. "Tell me you haven't welcomed a cat into your family." Despite her best efforts, another sneeze exploded out of her. "Please."

"What's wrong with cats?" Violet wondered.

"Have I never told you that cats make my sister sneeze?" Ford asked.

"No!" Behind her spectacles, Violet's brown eyes looked horrified. "Why didn't you?"

"They used to affect me just a little bit." Kendra's eyes were beginning to itch. "But lately—"

"How could we let this happen?" Violet exclaimed over Kendra's fourth sneeze. "I'm so sorry! I fear Rebecca has begun collecting stray cats. Her Aunt Lily heartily approves, but—"

"Rebecca!" Ford interrupted, rising from the couch where he sat beside Violet. He shouted their daughter's name again up the stairs, then climbed the wooden treads two at a time to fetch her.

"Dear heavens," Kendra said and sneezed yet again.

"I'm sorry!" Violet repeated.

Kendra sneezed three more times before Ford returned with eleven-year-old Rebecca in tow. With her dark hair and bright blue eyes, she was most definitely her father's daughter. But the two of them were in clear disagreement.

"I'll say this one last time," he told her. "You must keep your cats outdoors for the duration of your Aunt Kendra's visit." Leaning over the back of a couch, he snatched up an orange tabby and strode to the entrance hall.

Kendra heard the door open and shut and assumed he'd tossed it outside.

"Find the rest and put them outside, too," he added as he returned to the drawing room. "How many do you have now?"

"T-ten. But Papa, it's cold outside!"

"Ten cats?" Kendra blinked her irritated eyes. "*Ten* cats? Who on earth lives with *ten* cats?"

Rebecca put her hands on her hips, which were clad in an adorable sapphire-blue gown, an exact miniature of her mother's. "Aunty Lily has twelve."

"Or thirteen," Violet put in. "We're never quite sure. The number varies."

The orange tabby reappeared on a windowsill—the

one belonging to the only window that had been left slightly open—and let loose a long, sad *meow*. It squeezed inside, leapt to the floor, and promptly ran to Rebecca, who swept it up into her arms. "It's all right, Kitty," the girl crooned. "It's too cold out there, I know."

Kendra sneezed again and blew her nose. Loudly. From upstairs, two more sneezes resounded, one after the other.

"Are some of the children ill?" Amy asked.

"Not ill," Trick said grimly. "Cats make Cas and Pol sneeze as well."

"Oh, no," Violet breathed. "The cats have been all over this house. Where will everyone sleep?"

"Those affected by cats will sleep in the cottage, quite obviously," Ford said. "I must say, I didn't expect to be nearly this happy we finally renovated that old place."

Violet nodded. "We must rearrange everyone and have this house scoured clean. Jason, would you and Cait mind moving in here so Kendra and Trick can have your cottage bedchamber?" She turned to Kendra. "Our first arrivals chose the more peaceful rooms, since it's bound to be chaos in here, but—"

"Of course we'll move," Jason interrupted as he rose. "And Griffin and Adam will move in here, too, so their cottage chamber can go to Cas and Pol. I'll instruct our staff to transfer our things immediately," he added, striding from the room to see it done.

"Kitty needs to go outside, Rebecca." Taking the cat from his daughter's arms, Ford opened the window wider, then tossed the animal back outdoors before slamming the sash down with a resounding *bang*. "And the rest of them, too. Otherwise there will be nowhere we can all gather together."

"It's too cold for my kitties to be outside all day and night!" Pathetic meowing came through the mottled glass, and Rebecca began to cry. "They'll die! And it will be all *your* fault!"

Violet rose and went to pat her daughter on the back. "There, there, dear. They cannot stay in here, or Aunty Kendra and Cas and Pol won't be able to join in our festivities."

"We can gather in the cottage!" Rebecca more or less bellowed.

"No, we cannot," Ford returned. "There are"— Kendra could all but see her twin brother's brain whirl as he calculated—"twenty-one of us who need to gather." He paused and blinked. "Bloody hell, how did we get to be so many?"

"We all had children," Violet informed him calmly before turning back to her daughter. "Your kitties don't have to stay outdoors. You may keep them in the stables, so long as you remember to go feed them and enlist the help of the stableboys to make sure they don't escape."

Kendra was sneezing *and* wheezing now, and two

more sneezes resounded from upstairs, nearly in concert.

"But—"

"No buts, Rebecca," Ford interrupted. "Your mother has proposed a reasonable solution. Go upstairs and ask your cousins to help you find the remaining cats. All of your cousins except Cas and Pol, that is."

"I'll let Hilda know she needs to recruit every hand to clean." Violet followed her daughter upstairs.

As Jason returned, wrapped in a warm cloak, Kendra sneezed yet again.

Amy rose. "Kendra, let's go to the cottage. You can return when all the cats have been removed and the house has been swept."

Kendra looked to her husband. "Trick?"

"We men should go cut the Yule Log," Jason said. "Our belongings are being transferred now. I trust you ladies can oversee moving everyone."

"Amy, did you bring the plum pudding?" Cait asked.

"Of course," Colin said. "And speaking of plum pudding, I'm hungry. We've been waiting for Kendra for dinner."

"You and your Chase stomach," Amy said with a little huff. "It's barely past noon. Now you'll wait while the cats are removed so Kendra can join us in the dining room."

"We'll choose the Yule Log, then we'll have dinner,

then we'll light the log," Ford said. "Which will begin our celebrations."

"Good plan," Caithren said as an army of servants began to troop in, armed with buckets, mops, brooms, and rags. "Because God knows we certainly aren't cele-bratory now."

Jason headed toward the entry hall. "Let's go."

Kendra looked beseechingly toward Trick, who just shrugged as he followed her brothers outside. She sneezed a particularly pathetic sneeze, hoping he would hear it and feel guilty that he was leaving her to go cut a stupid log.

Never mind that she loved Christmas.

"Come along." Amy drew her in the opposite direc-tion, through the house.

"I'll come too," Cait said, jumping up to follow them. "I want to make sure all my things are moved out."

The three of them went through a side door and into a courtyard, across which stood the newly renovated "cottage," which was actually a three-story house built of sturdy stone.

"It's not that cold out here," Kendra muttered, still wrapped in her own cloak since she'd never even both-ered to sit down. "The blasted cats won't die. They're wild animals, for heaven's sake."

Shivering in just her gown, Amy chuckled as they crossed the courtyard, each step making crunching sounds on the snow-encrusted grass. "The cottage turned out lovely. You're lucky to be sneezing so you can stay here. Did you know it used to be called the Priest's House, back when the property was owned by a monastery?"

"Fascinating," Kendra said sarcastically.

Amy opened the door and led her into a bright common room. It had a table surrounded by six chairs, plus extra seating that looked plush and comfortable. Everything smelled fresh and new, which should have pleased Kendra—except nothing could please her right now.

"See, they forgot our backgammon set," Cait exclaimed, gesturing to where it sat on the table. "I knew they'd forget something."

Kendra couldn't bring herself to care.

"Look here," Amy said cheerfully. "They removed the old kitchen and added a bedchamber there instead."

An open door on the right revealed a room with two single beds. Cait peeked inside. "Well, at least they've moved all of Griffin's and Adam's things. Cas and Pol will have this room now." She turned to start up the wooden staircase.

Amy drew Kendra after her. "There are three beautiful new bedchambers upstairs. Jewel is staying in the smallest one—as the oldest cousin, she's been granted the luxury of her own room. And the attic is partitioned into four chambers where all of our staff will sleep."

"Fascinating," Kendra repeated.

Halfway up the stairs, Amy stopped and swiveled to her. "Why do you seem so vexed? Surely it cannot just be the cats."

"My apologies." Belatedly realizing she was acting beastly, Kendra sighed. Her dear sisters-in-law deserved better. "I'm not happy that Trick isn't here."

"But he is here." A frown appeared between Amy's dark brows. "He's helping choose the Yule Log."

Cait nodded. "Did you want to be doing that instead? It *is* fun—"

"No, that's not it." Clasping her hands together in frustration, Kendra decided to confide in the two best friends she had. "Trick is here, but he's not *here*." Her knuckles were turning white. "He was gone for more than nine weeks—over two months!—and he just returned in the middle of the night. And then we had to come here…before we even managed to make love! And it's not that we haven't tried—"

"Do stop," interrupted a deep voice from below. "I'd rather not hear about my sister's love life."

With a gasp, Amy whirled. "Well, then you shouldn't be eavesdropping. You're supposed to be choosing the Yule Log."

At the bottom of the stairs, Colin backed away, his hands held up defensively. "I returned for my cloak."

"Then get it and get out."

Colin just looked at her for a long, tense moment.

"Very well, then," he finally bit out.

The women plastered themselves against the wall as he rushed up the stairs and disappeared, then hurried back down and out the door, his cloak streaming behind him.

"Wheesht," Cait said after the door had slammed. She looked to Amy. "What's between you two?"

"Nothing," Amy said shortly, pushing past her and up the stairs to the landing.

Turning toward the left, she disappeared from view. Kendra and Cait exchanged a meaningful glance before following her up and then through a door at the far end of the corridor.

"This is the room Jason and I just vacated," Cait explained. "It's the largest one and on the end, so it has the most windows."

The chamber boasted pale green walls, a four-poster bed with rich blue hangings, and a carved wood washstand, wardrobe cabinet, and dressing table. A big chest rested at the foot of the bed, and an octagonal table with two deep green velvet-upholstered chairs sat beneath one of the five modern sash windows. Everything looked new.

"Kendra, look at this pretty chamber," Amy said way too brightly. "You and Trick will surely have a lovely reunion here."

In unison, Kendra and Cait dropped to sit on the big feather bed. "Tell us," Cait said.

It was Amy's turn to sigh. She began pacing. "Colin and I are having a little disagreement."

"About?" Kendra prompted.

"He promised me—before Jewel was even born—he *promised* me that our second son would reestablish my father's company, Goldsmith & Sons. It's time for Aidan to be apprenticed to properly learn his trade, to learn the business of running a shop. But Aidan doesn't want to do that. And Colin is supporting his view, never mind that *he promised me*."

"And a Chase promise is never given lightly," Cait quoted softly.

"Exactly," Amy gritted out, still pacing back and forth.

Kendra wondered how long it might take to wear grooves into a brand-new polished wood floor. "What does Aidan want to do instead?"

"He says he has no notion." Looking disgusted, Amy brushed at her lavender skirts. "He's a remarkably talented goldsmith—even more talented than I, which takes some doing, I'll have you know. But he says he doesn't want to spend his life making jewelry."

"He's only fifteen," Cait pointed out. "Maybe he'll change his mind."

"When? When he's twenty-five? When it's too late to find an apprenticeship, because guild members expect to train children, not full-grown men? It's nearly too late to apprentice him already." With a huff, Amy stopped moving and turned to look at them both. "Besides, the real point here isn't what Aidan wants, it's that Colin is taking his side against me. After he *promised*."

"It's true that Chase promises are not given lightly," Kendra allowed. "But can you not put this aside for Christmas? It's *Christmas*, Amy."

Amy winced. "You're right, and I promised Colin I'd put it aside, too. I should do so. My apologies." She blew out a long breath, visibly calming herself.

Violet walked in, looking much too cheerful. "Are you all getting settled in here?"

"As settled as can be expected," Kendra said dryly.

"I am *so* sorry about the cats." Violet's false cheer disappeared as she sighed. "I swear I feel nearly as miserable as you do."

"You don't know the half of it," Amy muttered.

Plastering a stiff smile on her face, Kendra looked to Caithren. "Well. At least one of us is happy."

A puzzled frown crossed Violet's features as a long silence ensued.

Glancing between her three English sisters, Cait finally broke it. "I'm not happy. I'm terrified."

"What?" the other three said together.

"Why?" Kendra added with concern.

Cait moved her hands to rest on the pointed bottom of her stomacher. "I'm carrying a bairn."

More silence reigned over the pretty new blue-and-green room until Kendra caught her breath. "Oh my

God, that's wonderful!" she gushed, wondering if it really was wonderful.

"Is it?" Cait's voice sounded strained. "I'm forty-three. Jamie's fourteen years old."

"But you're having a babe. How can a babe not be wonderful?" Long past pacing, Amy plopped to sit on her other side.

Violet knelt at Cait's feet. "And you're healthy," she added. "What does Jason think?"

"He doesn't know."

"What?" they all repeated.

"I just figured it out this morning—God's truth, I counted the days on my calendar seven times before I believed it. There were other signs, but it still seemed it couldn't be true." Cait dropped her head and covered her face with her hands. "Now I'm afraid to tell him," came muffled through her fingers. "I'm going to wait till after Christmas."

"Oh, no," Kendra said, wrapping an arm around Cait's shoulders. "You must tell him now. It's not fair to keep news like this to yourself."

"I cannot. I...I just cannot. Every time I think of doing so, I feel like I'm going to boak."

"To what?"

"To boak. To puke, to vomit, to—"

"That's the morning sickness," Amy interrupted. She wrapped an arm around Cait, too. "For heaven's sake, why should you be scared to tell him?"

Cait's hands dropped to her lap, but her words were still directed there. "He wants to travel to Scotland next summer, just the two of us—he's so happy that our lads are finally old enough for us to leave them. He was planning to ask you and Colin if Adam and James could stay with you for a month next year—" Breaking off, she looked up at Amy.

"Of course. Of course they are welcome to stay at Greystone anytime. I'd be pleased to have them, and I'm sure Colin would be, too."

"But can't you see? We cannot do that with a new bairn! We cannot travel to Scotland in July with a bairn due in August or September. Twenty years he's waited for this, and we'll be restarting that count from one! He's so happy now, and he'll be so upset. I cannot tell him now—I just cannot! I cannot ruin his Christmas."

Violet reached up to grab her hands and hold them tight. "You have to tell him, Cait. You must, and not only because it's the right thing to do. Keeping this secret and dreading his response will ruin *your* Christmas."

"And his response will be a relief." Kendra squeezed Cait's shoulder. "I know my brother—he won't be upset. He'll be happy."

"You think so, aye?" Cait snorted. "The last time the possibility of another child was mentioned, he called the notion a *calamity*."

The other three women exchanged glances. "I'm sure

he didn't mean it the way it sounds," Amy said carefully.

"I'm sure, too," Kendra added. "A new babe, Cait… it's a blessing. Maybe you'll finally have your girl."

A shaky laugh escaped Cait's lips. "Somehow I doubt I'll be that lucky."

"But you'll tell him, won't you? For your sake as well as his. It's tearing you up inside—I can tell. You cannot keep this from him."

"Today," Amy added. "You must tell him today."

"Very well." Cait swallowed hard. "I'll tell him."

"Today?" Violet pressed.

"Today."

EIGHT

COLIN

"IT FITS," Jason said when the men had finished wrestling the Yule Log into the drawing room's huge fireplace.

"I told you it would." Ford wiped his hands on his breeches. "When will you all learn to trust my ability to judge area? Perhaps by the next century?"

Colin rolled his eyes. "Yes, it fits—but barely."

"If it fit with room to spare, it wouldn't last through the holiday." Ford looked to Trick. "Did you bring the brand?"

They always lit the log with a brand saved from the previous year's log—it was one of their many traditions. Since Trick and Kendra had hosted last Christmas, it was up to them to bring the brand they'd set aside.

Trick shrugged. "I got home in the middle of the night. I assume Kendra took care of that. I'll go ask her."

"I'm ravenous," Ford said, "and Hilda is putting dinner on the table. Don't be long."

They all set off, Ford and Jason going upstairs to fetch their wives and children while Trick and Colin headed outdoors and crossed the courtyard to the cottage.

"Yours will be the chamber at end of the corridor," Colin said, leading Trick up the staircase. "I assume Jason and Cait's things will have been swapped for yours by now."

After watching his brother-in-law walk off, Colin entered the closer chamber, wondering whether to be apprehensive or pleased when he found Amy there.

"Hey," he said softly, then added, "I'm sorry," even though he wasn't sure what he was sorry for.

He only knew he wanted her to be happy.

He wanted them to be happy together.

"I'm sorry, too." Rising from where she was seated at a small parquet table with two red-velvet chairs, Amy came close. "I know I said I'd be agreeable for Christmas, and I meant that. Please forgive me."

He moved closer and gathered her into his arms. Though he wished things were really right between them, temporarily right was better than not right at all. He gave her a gentle kiss, then smiled when she wrapped her arms around his neck and laid her head upon his chest.

This room had cream walls, red bedhangings, and only one window, but it was otherwise quite similar to the one next door. "Thin walls in this place," he observed, hearing the murmur of conversation from the larger chamber.

"We cannot tell what they're saying," Amy pointed out. "Their voices are muffled."

"Thank heaven for small favors. As I said, I don't want to hear about my sister's love life."

The adjacent room went suddenly silent. Half a minute later, when they heard a muted moan from Kendra, Amy giggled. "I think I know what they're doing."

"Bloody hell. I don't want to hear *that*, either."

"At this point, I suspect your dear sister doesn't care," Amy returned with a laugh that lifted his heart.

He didn't want to be at odds with her.

But he *really* didn't want to hear his sister make love with her husband.

Dropping a kiss on Amy's forehead, he left the room and went down the corridor to knock on Kendra's door.

"Time for dinner!" he called more loudly than necessary.

The moan he heard next had an entirely different tone. Kendra stomped over and opened the door. "A pox on you. I'm not hungry."

"Well, I am." He noted with some relief that she hadn't yet removed any clothing. "And everyone's waiting."

"A pox on everyone, then," she said. "When will this family learn patience?"

Colin looked past her to Trick and was relieved to see him fully dressed as well. "How about you?" he asked. "Are you hungry?"

"He's a man," Amy called out from down the corridor, and they all laughed.

Well, all of them except Kendra.

As the two couples trooped down the stairs and outside—Amy calling "Dinnertime, Jewel!" as they passed her chamber—Kendra maneuvered herself beside Colin so she could elbow him in the ribs.

"Oof!" he said good-naturedly. He was entirely too busy planning a prank to pay her any mind.

It had come to him in a single bolt of inspiration, conceived upon hearing the words *"When will this family learn patience?"* spoken so very impatiently. The mere concept had lifted his spirits immensely.

Given the way things were going, he sorely needed some fun, and this stunt was going to be more than fun.

It was going to be hilarious.

❄

*D*INNER featured salmon pie, capon in orange sauce, stewed cucumbers, turnip pudding, and apple tart. Colin cleaned his plate without tasting much of anything. He was completely focused on plotting his prank.

It was going to be *more* than hilarious.

He couldn't wait to get started.

After the meal, when the family lit the Yule Log, it seemed to take much longer than ever before in his memory. Just getting twenty-one people out of the dining room and gathered by the fireplace proved to be an exercise in patience. Kendra couldn't locate the brand, necessitating a search. By the time it appeared, three of the youngsters had wandered off and needed to be fetched. Then the log, which was damp, took an absurd amount of time to set ablaze. And when did their little family ceremony become so lengthy and elaborate?

Colin wanted to punch a wall.

Once the Yule Log was lit, it took another eternity to organize everyone to play hot-cockles, a simple game where a blindfolded family member tried to guess who tapped him on the back. To avoid arousing suspicion, Colin cheerfully participated through five rounds, considering himself a veritable model of self-restraint.

Finally, his turn arrived. As Ford's son Nicky tied the blindfold over his eyes, Colin mentally crossed his fingers, hoping this would be his chance. Before too long, someone tapped him on the back. Her rose scent was the giveaway that allowed him to identify her immediately.

"Amy!" he crowed, grabbing her and pulling her down to his lap.

She giggled.

Pleased that she'd chosen him, he whipped off his mask. "I'll be back," he whispered, feeling a combination of glee and relief as he got to his feet and set her aside. "I have a special surprise for you."

Her grin made his heart swell. Never mind that he didn't have a surprise already planned. He'd needed an excuse to get away, and he'd find a surprise before he returned.

Leaving the circle, he plucked his cloak off a peg on the wall.

"Where are you going?" Jason asked.

"To the cottage, because my wife deserves an early Christmas gift." He headed toward the side door. "I won't be long."

Free at last, he hurried across the courtyard to the cottage and upstairs to Kendra's chamber, hoping her maid would be inside.

Well, actually, hoping her maid would be at Lakefield at all. With four families in residence at once, Violet had requested they all bring minimum staff only, as there simply wasn't room for three full sets of extra servants. He and Amy had brought his valet, Benchley, but not her lady's maid.

When he opened the door, he was pleased to see Kendra's maid inside as he'd hoped. Small and slight, she wore a simple brown dress over a long-sleeved linen shift. In the midst of reading a book, she gasped and jumped up from where she was seated at the dressing table. "My apologies, my lord. I think your chamber is next door?"

"Indeed, it is. But it is you I wish to see, Miss...?"

"Margaret." Still holding her book, she tucked a stray lock of russet hair back under her cap. "What can I do for you, Lord Greystone?"

He wondered how she knew who he was, but supposed Kendra had told her. Or perhaps knowing such things was simply a part of her job.

"I'm hoping you'll be willing to help me play a prank on my sister."

Her blue eyes widened. "I cannot play a prank on my mistress! I mean...my apologies, my lord, but I cannot do that."

"Are you certain?" Gauging her interest, he walked a little closer. "I would never harm my sister—what I have in mind is just for fun. Would five pounds make the prospect more palatable?"

"No! Absolutely not! I owe everything to her grace. And his grace." She swallowed hard, evidently tempted by five pounds but determined to resist. "I grew up at Caldwell Manor."

"Did you, now?" Caldwell Manor was Trick's orphanage. "I trust you were treated well there?"

"Extremely well. I was five when they took me in." Her chin went up. "It was the luckiest day of my life."

That was doubtlessly true. The children at Caldwell Manor were well fed and uncommonly well educated. Not every lady's maid spent her spare hours reading books—indeed, most maids couldn't read at all. Colin was unsurprised to find that Margaret was loyal to Kendra.

However, loyalty went only so far. "Ten pounds?"

"Ten pounds? Lud…" She set her book on the dressing table as she plopped to sit on the stool there. "I…I couldn't."

He could see her weakening. "Twenty pounds, then." It was a pittance to him, but four years' wages for a servant. "And that's my final offer."

At first she shook her head slowly. But when a tiny, rueful smile emerged along with an even tinier shrug, he knew he had won.

*H*ALF AN hour later, Colin returned to where the family was still playing games.

"What took you so long?" Jason asked.

"I went to my chamber to fetch this"—Colin held up a thick book—"and saw a mouse."

"A mouse?" Amy squealed.

He'd known she would squeal. Amy hated mice with an illogical passion.

Almost as much as she hated horses.

"There's no need to worry, love. I went and found some traps and set up a few in our chamber. That's what took me so long—finding the mousetraps, mostly. I had to locate some servants to help me find them." He looked to Kendra. "Your maid—what is her name?"

"Margaret."

"Right. She's setting some traps in your room, too, and other servants are busy covering the rest of the cottage. You won't see any mice."

Violet looked horrified. "I'm so sorry you saw a mouse."

"I had no idea there were mice in the cottage," Ford added with a frown.

"How could you know?" Colin sent his brother an understanding smile. "I presume you haven't stayed in the cottage yourself. In any case, it's all taken care of and no harm done." He waved a hand in dismissal. "Here, love," he added, handing Amy the book. "Here's the early Christmas gift I promised."

It was bound in tan leather with a gold-stamped design on the front. *The History of the World* by Sir

Walter Raleigh!" she exclaimed in delight. "How did you know I wanted this?"

He hadn't known, precisely—but since Amy happily devoured nearly every book she managed to get her hands on, it had been a safe bet.

"I have a copy of that book in a quite similar binding," Violet marveled. Most books didn't come bound— owners typically purchased the pages and had covers made to their preferences. "How astonishing!"

"Hmm, isn't it?" Colin murmured, although of course it wasn't astonishing at all, considering he'd found the book in Violet's own library.

Unfortunately, he'd had no choice but to take it.

After enlisting Margaret's help with setting up his prank, he'd gone in search of a surprise for Amy and hit dead ends at every turn.

First he'd looked in the room he and Amy had been assigned, but found nothing he could give her besides the Christmas gift he'd brought, which he couldn't give to her now—he had to save it for Christmas Eve. Nothing else in his luggage seemed at all appropriate, and though the room itself was fresh and pretty (and mouse-free), it had offered nothing in the way of last-minute gifts. He'd found naught in the rest of the building, either. Recently remodeled, it was pristine and had yet to accumulate any clutter.

Flowers, he'd decided as he'd left the cottage. She'd doubtless love some flowers. But he'd gone outdoors and all around the house and found no flowers. Of course, it was late December. Although it wasn't snowing now, a layer of snow covered everything. And it was cold. Apparently too cold for flowers.

Next he'd sneaked in the side entrance of the main house and stolen upstairs, where again he'd found nothing appropriate. Nothing in any of the bedrooms, nothing in Ford and Violet's dressing room. Ford's laboratory had been locked, but Colin figured Amy wouldn't want a beaker, thermometer, or microscope anyway.

No, what Amy liked was books, he'd finally realized…

Which was how he'd ended up in Violet's library. He'd had to go back outside and all the way around the house to the front entrance in order to get into the library undetected. But it had been worth the cold and the trouble, because there, among a plethora of philosophy tomes, he'd found *The History of the World*.

Amy loved all books, but she loved history books best, so it had seemed a good choice.

Judging by Amy's excitement, it had been a grand choice indeed. He would simply replace Violet's copy before she noticed it was missing. He'd found the book on a bottom shelf—surely Violet rarely looked there—and made note of the publisher on a piece of paper he'd snitched from her desk and now had in his pocket.

The book's front page had proclaimed it was

"Printed by William Stansby for Walter Burre, and sold at his shop in Paules Church-yard at the signe of the Crane in London." The fact that it had been printed decades ago was but a minor inconvenience. Although Sir Walter Raleigh had been dead some seventy years, he was still a popular author—surely Colin would be able to find another copy of the book the next time he went to the City.

"What a lovely gift," Kendra said to Amy now. "Is anyone else tired? I'm exhausted."

"I need to finish making my gifts." Jewel rose and stretched. "Uncle Ford, have you any wire I can use? I fear I may not have brought enough."

"Of course," Ford said. "Come up to my laboratory."

"I really am tired," Kendra repeated more loudly. "I think I fancy a nap before supper."

Everyone turned to look at her. Colin raised a brow. "A nap?"

"Yes, a nap," she snapped out.

A nap. Ha. He rather thought she fancied taking her husband to bed. Just let her try, he thought, hard put to keep a grin off his face.

"I'm weary, too," Trick said. "I got home in the middle of the night."

"So we heard." Colin waved a magnanimous hand. "Run along, you two. And Jewel. Anyone staying here want to play cards?"

NINE

KENDRA

OUT OF BREATH after dashing to their chamber, Kendra and Trick barely took time to shut the door before locking their lips together.

In no time at all, Kendra went from out of breath to downright woozy. Her head spun. Her heart raced. Her husband's arms were around her, and he smelled like—

"What on earth is that smell?" she gasped, pulling away.

"What smell?" Trick yanked her back against him. "You smell lovely. Delightful. Like—"

"Like fifty pairs of smelly stockings!" She held her nose, but that didn't help. "It's awful. Can you not smell it?"

He sniffed at the air. "I suppose. But do I care? No.

Hearts wounds, I've missed you." He pressed his mouth to hers again, urgently, one arm holding her close while the other began hiking up her skirts.

She'd missed him, too. She wanted to do this.

She made an effort to sink into the kiss, to immerse herself in the sensation of Trick's deft lips moving on hers, his fingers skimming over her silk-stockinged leg, his solid body and strong arm holding her up. A tingling warmth began to grow within her, over-whelming conscious thought, replacing it with unthink-ing, unbridled physical need.

For all of five seconds.

"Ugh!" She broke the kiss. "I cannot stand it! It's *worse* than fifty pairs of smelly stockings! It's like a hundred rotten eggs! It's like—"

"Bloody hell," he interrupted, releasing her and step-ping away. "I'll open the windows." Stalking over to the longest wall, he shoved up the top panels of the newfan-gled sash windows. "There. Better?"

"Now I'm cold."

"I'll warm you up in no time," he said, crossing back to her and dragging her back into his arms. "Sweet Mary, *leannan*, I cannot wait—"

"Wait! Oh, my God, wait!" Spotting something on the floor beneath the bed, she pulled away to retrieve it. "A mousetrap." She sniffed at it. "Set with the most awful-smelling cheese imaginable!"

It was a soft cheese. Hunting around the chamber,

she found more of it smeared here and there, near where other traps were set. Along the windowsill, beneath the bed, across the top of the headboard. Exasperated, she threw back the counterpane, shrieking when she found traps in the bedding too.

"Who in their right mind puts mouse traps in a bed?"

Trick shrugged. "Colin said he saw mice in here. Someone must have got overzealous. Maybe Margaret."

"We should have brought Edmund instead. He might have some common sense."

"Don't be so hard on the lass. She's only trying to help." He swiped the traps off the bed and onto the floor. "There. They're gone." Grabbing her hand, he pulled her onto the mattress, falling with her and wrapping his arms around her tightly.

But not so tightly that she couldn't escape. She leapt to her feet, holding her nose. "I cannot make love with this stench in the room! I'm going to find Margaret. She'll need to toss all the mousetraps, air the room, and change the bedding. I vow and swear, I'd rather deal with mice than this stink."

The expression on Trick's face made her stifle a laugh. She couldn't remember ever seeing him pout before, but he was pouting now, reminding her of a disappointed little boy. "Are you certain?" he asked.

She hesitated, the last of the tingling warmth still lingering in her middle. Her husband was sprawled on the bed, his silky-straight blond hair mussed, his snow-white shirt untucked, his gorgeous amber eyes imploring her. He looked better than dessert.

On her next inhale, she was certain.

"I'm certain." So certain she walked to the door, threw it open, and headed to the attic to find Margaret—because she really couldn't tolerate the stench a moment longer.

"I'll meet you downstairs," she called back. "Let's gather the children and sing some carols. We'll try again tonight."

TEN

CAITHREN

"CAN WE SING 'Tyrley, Tyrlow' next?" Caithren's youngest son asked.

Without verbally acknowledging his request, Kendra returned her hands to the harpsichord and began playing the first notes of the familiar carol.

Cait smiled. After all these years with Jason, she had come to adore Christmas with his family, even though she still missed her cousin Cameron and their own traditions during this season. She especially loved how enthusiastic her three lads were this time of year. Her heart seemed to swell as their voices rose in song.

"I pray you all that be here

For to sing and make good cheer
In the worship of God this year
Tyrley, tyrlow, tyrley, tyrlow, tyrley, tyrlow…"

Would the new bairn grow up to love Christmas, too? For a moment, she imagined herself at Cainewood this same day next year, holding her wee babe wrapped in the Leslie tartan she'd been saving, rocking the bairn in time to this same carol, sniffing the sweet newborn scent in its downy hair…

As a wee bit of excitement pushed through her anxiety, she smiled again.

Amy leaned close. "Have you told Jason yet?" she whispered.

Cait shook her head. Crivvens, she had to tell him. "I will," she whispered back.

"Before supper?"

"Before supper."

She had to find a way. And *he* wouldn't be smiling.

"Ahem."

Kendra's fingers paused on the harpsichord's keyboard. Everyone stopped singing and looked to Hilda, Lakefield's elderly housekeeper. She smoothed her hands over the wide white apron that covered her yellow cotton frock.

"Supper will be served in half an hour," she announced.

"Oh, we should all ready ourselves," Violet said as she rose. "We can sing more carols after supper."

"I'm ready already," Rebecca announced, jumping up. "I'm going to check on my kitties." She ran through the room and to the side door.

A moment later, her high-pitched voice drifted back. "Oh, it's snowing!"

Her twin, Marcus, bolted for the door, while their older sibling and cousins followed. Feeling no need to view the snow, Caithren stayed put.

"Come." Jason held out a hand to help her rise. "Let's spruce up."

She stood and trailed him up the stairs, bracing herself.

She could do this.

When they reached the bedchamber they were using, a pretty pink room that normally belonged to Rebecca, she steeled her nerves. "Jase, there's something I need to tell you."

"Oh, yes?" He drew her inside and into his arms, pushing the door closed behind them. "There's something I need to tell *you*." He kissed her softly. "I missed you all day today—I missed being alone with you." Tenderly he brushed the hair back from her face, making a little shiver run through her. "I cannot wait till the summer, when we can be alone for weeks and weeks. I was thinking we might ride ahead of the baggage train, just the two of us, and visit some of the places we stayed before we were married. Like the place in Stilton where we had our first kiss—"

"Actually, our first kiss was in Newark, though you don't remember it. You were asleep."

Jason chuckled. "Right, we'll stop there too." He kissed the end of her nose, a silly smile on his face. "I feel like a schoolboy looking forward to term break."

Cait bit her lip. "I thought you never went to school." The Civil War and its aftermath had robbed him of the chance—of all the Chase siblings, only Ford had received any education outside the home. "How would you know how a schoolboy feels?" she asked, knowing she was blethering to delay telling him about the bairn.

"Very well, I feel like I *imagine* a schoolboy feels," he returned with another little chuckle. Then he gathered her closer and kissed her again, more deeply.

Twenty-one years into their marriage, this was unexpected in the middle of the day. Unexpected and delightful. Taking advantage, she wrapped her arms around his neck and surrendered to the moment. As she concentrated on him—his spicy scent, his soft lips and tongue, all familiar yet endlessly exciting—her resolve seemed to fade away.

"What did you want to tell me?" he asked when he finally pulled back.

Her heart was racing.

Bloody hell, she remembered him saying, *you're not with child, are you? What a calamity that would be!*

"Jase, I…"

Her courage failed her.

"I wanted to tell you I cannot breathe in this dress," she continued with a wee forced laugh. "Will you loosen the laces a smitch?"

"But of course," he replied with a grin, no doubt thinking she could easily do so herself.

While he removed her stomacher, he began humming the tune that went with "Tyrley, Tyrlow." She drew a deep breath and focused on the dancing flames in the fireplace. Maybe he would notice her *pleasingly plump* breasts again and ask her if she might really be with child. Though she couldn't find the words to tell him, it would be easier to simply confirm his suspicions.

After loosening and retying her laces, he replaced her stomacher, stripped off his shirt, splashed water on his face, and washed his hands, all while still cheerfully humming.

She watched him comb the long wavy hair she still loved even though it was now streaked with more than a few strands of silver.

Still humming.

So much for him noticing anything. He was so happy looking forward to time away together. How could she tell him that wouldn't be happening? How could she ruin his Christmas?

She didn't have the strength.

"I'm feeling strangely fatigued," she said as he donned a fresh shirt. "I think I'll lie down for a few minutes before supper."

She'd sometimes felt fatigued during her three pregnancies. Maybe he'd remember that and ask her if she might be carrying.

He shrugged back into his surcoat. "Do you want me to stay with you?"

"Nay, go ahead. I'll be down in a few minutes."

"As you wish," he said, then kissed her again and left.

Dejected, she did lie down for a while, her mind racing.

She had to tell him.

She'd tell him after supper.

When a knock came at the door, she rose and opened it to find her brother-in-law Colin on the other side.

"You look lovely," he said perfunctorily, without even looking her over.

Which was fine with her. She didn't want anyone noticing her expanded bosom before she found the mettle to tell Jason the truth.

"Thank you," she said just as perfunctorily. "Jason is downstairs already."

"I'm not looking for him." He followed her inside. "Did you bring any herbal remedies with you?"

"Of course. What's ailing you?"

"It's not for me. I'm hoping you might have something to help Aidan sleep."

"Why can't he sleep?" She crossed to the wooden case she always carried with her. "Griffin and Adam both slept like the dead at fifteen."

"The poor lad is so worried about being shipped off as an apprentice that he's waking with nightmares every hour."

"Oh. I heard about this from Amy." In the middle of opening the case's lid, she paused to glance up at him. "Your promise."

"Yes, my cursed promise. Which I should never have made." He looked downright miserable. "I certainly wasn't anticipating condemning my son to a life he'd hate when I made that promise."

"I'm sure you weren't. And Aidan shouldn't be forced." She began pulling out various vials. "It's his life, not Amy's."

"Will you tell her that? Because I can talk to her till I'm blue in the face, but—"

"I'll talk to her. I'm not sure she'll listen, but I'll talk. Ah, here it is. Valerian." She uncorked a vial and grabbed a tiny drawstring bag. "You'll need only a wee pinch," she said, putting a bit of the ground dried root into it.

"How is Aidan supposed to take this?"

"Add it to a hot drink and give it to him before bed." She pulled the drawstring closed. "Does he like ale?"

"What boy his age doesn't?"

"Indeed," she said with a little laugh. "Then put it in some warmed ale, because hops increase valerian's effectiveness. You could also add a little sugar and some ginger, nutmeg, and milk, to disguise the taste of the herb. That will make him more likely to finish it. Here." She handed him the valerian.

He sniffed at the little bag, grimaced, then opened it and sniffed again. "It smells like something died."

Caithren chuckled. "That's a fair enough description. And why I suggested sugar, ginger, nutmeg, and milk."

"Sugar, ginger, nutmeg, and milk," Colin repeated as though trying to memorize the list. "Can you give me some more? That way I won't have to bother you about this again tomorrow night. Actually, perhaps you should give me enough for use at home afterwards, until this matter is settled?"

"Sure, I have plenty." She uncorked the vial and dumped a little pile into the bag he held out. "Only one pinch per night, though," she warned. "A wee pinch, or else he'll sleep through the night and half of the next day, too."

His eyes widened in alarm. "It won't have any bad effects, will it? He'll be fine once he wakes up?"

"Of course. It's a harmless herb." She slid him a sharp glance. "I would never suggest you give your son —my nephew—anything at all dangerous. I was just cautioning you to use it responsibly."

"I understand, and I will." He slipped the tiny bag into his pocket.

"The others must be waiting downstairs for us by now. Shall we go?" Closing her wooden case, she licked her lips. "I hope they'll be serving plum pudding."

ELEVEN

JEWEL

"WOULD YOU like onion sauce on your venison, Lady Jewel? Or prune sauce?"

Jarred out of her thoughts, Jewel looked up at the footman. "Hmm, I cannot decide. May I have both on the side, please? Thank you."

As he spooned sauce onto her plate, she glanced around the enormous supper table—which was two tables set end-to-end, actually. All around her, family members were chatting cheerfully, enjoying their time together…completely unaware of the momentous decision she was facing.

Which had nothing to do with the trifling little matter of losing the maid she'd had her whole life.

Was it but yesterday that Henry Breckenridge, the

Viscount Copthorne, had asked her to marry him? She'd been able to think of little else since, making it feel as though a week or more had passed.

She'd promised an answer upon her return, which gave her just two more days to make up her mind. For the life of her, she couldn't fathom why this seemed to be such a wrenching decision. Henry was handsome, genteel, wealthy, and would someday be the Earl of Guildham. He treated her like a princess. The two of them got along well, and her parents liked him.

And yet she wasn't sure she wanted to wed him.

Well, in truth, Henry hadn't precisely asked for her hand—instead, he'd asked if she would entertain his offer before he approached her father for permission. Did that mean he was a little cowardly? Hmm, she wasn't sure. But she was grateful he'd come to her first, grateful he'd given her the chance to determine her own fate without her family interfering. Grateful enough that she'd kissed him.

Which she feared might have given him the wrong idea.

Still and all, it had been a nice kiss—

"Jewel, what do you think?" her mother interrupted.

"I cannot decide," she said, then realized no one knew what she meant.

She was grateful for that, too. The last thing she wanted was all their input.

Cousin Diana wrapped herself in a hug. "Well, I *can*

decide, and I've decided I'm scared."

"Scared of what?" Jewel asked, having no idea what they'd all been discussing.

"War," her brother Hugh said, looking much too thrilled at the prospect. "If King James continues to resist ceding the throne to William of Orange."

Papa rolled his eyes. "If I've told you once, Hugh, I've told you a dozen times"—Mama chimed in with him for the familiar refrain—"you are *not* going to war."

"Enough have lost their lives already," Aunty Caithren put in.

"Fewer than twenty," Uncle Jason pointed out.

"Even one lost life is tragic," their son Adam said. "If it comes to war—"

"It won't come to war," his older brother Griffin said, cutting him off. "Rumor has it that James is preparing to flee the country. And I believe William will permit that, to avoid making James a martyr for the Catholic cause."

Griffin was wise at age twenty. Jewel wondered if Henry were as wise at twenty-four. Did she know him well enough to marry him?

"I agree," Papa told Griffin. "It's in William's interest for people to think James left the country on his own, rather than having been forced or frightened into fleeing..."

Jewel's attention drifted off again, her gaze idly skimming the dining room's burgundy-painted walls and beautiful built-in cabinetry. Her siblings and cousins, all of them younger than she, seemed blissfully unaware of the pressure they'd face when they got to be her age. Although she was but one-and-twenty, her brothers teased her about her approaching spinsterhood. And every time she met a new eligible gentleman, her mother asked if she fancied wedding him.

She knew her immediate family would all want her to accept Lord Copthorne's proposal. Along with everyone else around the beautifully decorated holiday table. And his kisses were nice.

So why was it so hard to commit to marrying him?

Mama touched her hand. "You look like you're off in another world. What on earth have you been thinking about?"

"My Christmas gifts," Jewel fibbed. "They're all finished now, but I still need to wrap them."

"You have until tomorrow night. Join the conversation. Would you like some of this cake?"

She glanced down at the venison, creamed spinach, and cauliflower pudding on her plate, all of it untouched. She'd been too busy thinking to eat. "Not yet. Maybe later."

"I'll take some." Though she'd had a slice at the beginning of the meal, Aunty Kendra reached for the cake, surprising no one. "How about you, Cait?"

"Is there any plum pudding?"

"Well, yes," Aunty Violet said, "but we're saving it for tomorrow."

"Why is that?" Aunty Cait asked with a frown.

"Tradition," Mama told her. "We always serve it on Christmas Eve. To my mind, the flaming pudding signals the arrival of the holiday."

"Oh, aye? I hadn't noticed." Aunty Cait pulled a face. "As Kendra would say, a pox on tradition."

The cake plate was passed and the family continued chattering. Jewel took a few bites of her now-cold venison, thinking more about Henry. Did he love her? He'd said so, but in such a flowery, rehearsed manner, she couldn't help but wonder if his words had been sincere. And yet—

"What's wrong?" her father asked.

She was all set to say "Nothing" in a not-so-kind way, when she realized he hadn't been speaking to her. He'd addressed the question to Aunty Kendra, who was looking unusually glum.

"Nothing," Aunty Kendra snapped in the same not-so-kind way Jewel would have.

Jewel wondered what had predicated *that* odd exchange.

But not for long, because she couldn't help returning, once again, to the much larger conundrum of Henry's proposal.

How on earth was she—a girl who couldn't even make up her mind between onion sauce and prune sauce—supposed to decide her whole future in the next two days?

TWELVE

CAITHREN

*T*HE SKIES HAD cleared and the snow had ceased, leaving a fresh, soft blanket outdoors. The sounds of shouts and laughter drifted inside, making Caithren smile. Her two older sons had organized a snowball fight in the dark, by moonlight, with Jewel, Jewel's brothers, and Kendra's daughters. It was lads against lasses, and it seemed to Cait that the lasses were winning, even though they were outnumbered.

The Chases bred strong, clever women.

In the long dining room, the younger cousins were playing blowpoint: firing tiny paper balls through a peashooter, aiming toward a chalk target drawn on the wooden floor. Cait's son James was keeping score.

"Twelve points!" she heard him crow. "That's forty-two for you, Marc."

Warm and cozy by the fire in the vast drawing room, Ford and Jason were playing backgammon while the rest of the family chatted about food, the weather, their children, the future of the monarchy, and life in general. The conversation was pleasant but banal. Feeling restless, Caithren rose and wandered into the adjacent kitchen.

Amy followed her with a candle and began lighting the lamps on the stone walls. "What are you after, Cait? More mulled wine?"

"Oh, I'm just having a wee look around." Cait hadn't been sure what she was after when she headed in here, but suddenly she knew. "Wheesht, scratch that. I'm looking for plum pudding. I've been craving it for days —I can think of nothing else. I know it's not Christmas Eve yet, but I *must* have plum pudding."

"It's the child, you know." Amy chuckled as she drew a large pewter platter from the rack and set it on the wooden table in the center of the kitchen. "Your growing daughter is craving plum pudding."

"My daughter, aye?" Cait snorted. "The more you say that, the less I believe it. Where's the pudding?"

"I'm not hiding it, I swear." Amy crossed to a cupboard and fetched a large bowl while Cait found a spoon and took a plate from the freshly washed stack.

Kendra and Violet drifted in.

"What are you two doing in here?" Violet asked.

"Cait wants plum pudding." Amy uncovered the bowl and upended the pudding onto the platter. "She *must* have some. Or rather, her burgeoning babe must have some."

"It *does* look good." Always ready for a sweet, Kendra licked her lips. "It's glistening. It looks perfect this year, Amy."

"Well, it won't be perfect anymore," Cait declared. And with that, she grabbed a large knife and used it to carve a slice off the top of the domed pudding.

Violet gasped. "It was so pretty!"

"I'll fix it," Cait promised, plopping the slice onto the plate.

Kendra stared at the pudding in horror. "How?"

"I don't know." Cait spooned moist, delicious pudding into her mouth and sighed in pleasure. Why did she usually avoid plum pudding? What was wrong with her when she wasn't pregnant? "Maybe I'll decorate the top? There has to be some way to make it look like nothing was taken. Somehow, I'll fix it."

It was Amy's turn to snort. "It will be flaming when it's carried into the dining room, then taken away to be cut and served with the hard sauce I brought. No one will notice you had a pudding crisis, I assure you. What did Jason say when you told him?"

"I haven't. I'm a feartie."

Violet cocked her head. "A what?"

"A feartie—a coward. Oops!" Cait spit a small silver object into her hand. "I forgot there would be tokens in here."

"The wishbone, a sign of good luck." Taking it from her, Amy walked over to rinse it off under the innovative taps Ford had installed in his kitchen. "Maybe tonight you'll have better luck telling Jason."

Kendra watched Cait swallow the last bite. "Why haven't you told Jason?"

"I tried to, but..." Cait eyed the pudding. Sadly, another slice off the top would ruin it more obviously. She set down the spoon. "He was so happy, planning our journey to Scotland, imagining our days without children. I didn't want to disappoint him."

"He won't be disappointed." Amy carefully pushed the clean charm back inside the pudding for another family member to find. "Cait, you have to tell him." She covered the pudding and returned it to the cupboard. "Tonight."

"I will," Cait said. "Tonight. Can we talk about you now?"

Amy closed the cupboard and whirled to face her. "Me? Why should we talk about *me?*"

Caithren met her gaze straight on. "Because your son cannot sleep."

Amy narrowed her eyes as though she didn't understand. Then she blinked. "Aidan, you mean? You're talking about Aidan? Who told you he cannot sleep?"

"That doesn't signify." Cait didn't want to put Colin in the middle of this. "What matters is that he's having nightmares because he's so worried about being sent away. Or maybe *terrified* is a more accurate word than worried. You're not being fair to him."

Amy crossed her arms. "Life isn't fair. That shouldn't be news to anyone inhabiting this world. And he may be terrified now, but once he's apprenticed, he'll learn it's the life he's always been destined for. Aidan is *such* a talented goldsmith; I am certain this pursuit will make him happy once he embraces it." She paused for a breath. "And besides all of that, I vowed to my father that Goldsmith & Sons would not die with me. And Colin promised me it wouldn't."

"What Colin promised is beside the point. Aidan's life belongs to—"

"May I?" Kendra interrupted.

Since Amy didn't seem the least bit swayed, Cait was glad to nod her assent.

"Amy," Kendra said gently. "Will you listen to me for a moment? Really listen?"

"I'm listening," Amy all but snapped.

"Remember a long time ago, before the Great Fire of London?"

"Marry come up! Of course I remember. What of it?"

"I remember you telling me about your life with your father back then. How he loved you, but he didn't understand you. How he insisted you wed—what was his name? That apprentice?"

"Robert Stanley." Amy's lips quirked, making her look a tad less impatient. "You punched him in the face."

"That I did," Kendra recalled with a faint smile. "Anyhow, I remember you telling me how unfair it was, that your father was forcing you to marry a man you didn't like—a man you despised. How unfair it was that he was dictating your life instead of letting you live it."

Kendra paused for a moment, apparently waiting for Amy to respond.

But Amy didn't.

"Amy." Kendra reached to touch her arm. "Please listen. What your father did to you, well...you're doing the same thing to your own child—"

A sudden commotion erupted in the drawing room.

"The pond is frozen!" Caithren's middle son cried, having burst back into the house with his cousins. "It's so cold out there now! Can we go ice skating?"

"Now? It's nearly bedtime!" Hard put to keep from laughing, Cait emerged from the kitchen. "I think not."

"Tomorrow?"

"Did you ask anyone to pack your skates, Adam?"

"Oh." He looked so crestfallen, one might think his dog had died. "I didn't."

"Well, I didn't tell anyone to pack your skates, either. So it seems there will be no ice skating, aye?"

"Oh, yes, there will be."

Everyone turned to look at Ford.

"I was going to save this surprise for Christmas Eve, but..." Leaving that sentence unfinished, he bolted up the stairs and out of sight.

"Aunty Violet, what did Uncle Ford mean?" Pol asked.

"I haven't the slightest idea," she said blithely.

Too blithely. Cait suspected Violet knew exactly what Ford was up to.

They all held their collective breaths until he returned, carrying a huge basket filled with what looked to be oddly shaped gifts, all wrapped in bright-colored fabrics and tied with ribbons in every color of the rainbow. Violet's handiwork, if Cait didn't miss her guess.

"They're various different sizes." Ford set the basket in the middle of the drawing room and stepped back. "I suggest you each unwrap one and then swap to find a set that fits."

The cousins all converged in a rush. In no time, the floor was littered with scraps of fabric and ribbons, and they were all admiring their new skates and handing the larger pairs to the men.

"How do they work?" Cait asked, bemused. "These don't look like the skates we have at home. And why does each pair come with a key? What is that for?"

"The key is used to tighten the clamps, which attach the skate firmly to your shoes," Ford explained. "I think the clamps will work better than straps alone. At least, I hope they will."

"A brilliant invention, don't you think?" Behind their lenses, Violet's brown eyes danced. "As brilliant as the spectacles he made for me so many years ago!"

"Don't tell me you're going to patent this," Ford said with a half-groan.

Cait laughed, remembering when Ford had designed a new watch, and Violet had patented it before they'd even wed.

"No, darling," Violet said indulgently. "This time I'll leave that up to you."

"Which means it will never be patented," Kendra predicted. "Od's fish, I cannot remember ever being so tired. Thanks to smelly cheese, I missed my nap. I'm going to bed."

"I want to skate!" her daughter Diana protested.

"Tomorrow," Trick told her, already following his wife. "I'm off to bed, too."

"Good night," Violet called after them.

"But I want to skate!"

"Think, Diana." Her older sister Elspeth shook her head. "Use your brain. Do you really believe our parents will allow us to skate now, in the dark, at the pond out of view of the house? Let's go to our bedchamber and tell ghost stories."

The girls' "bedchamber" consisted of pallets on the

floor of Violet's library. "Good idea!" Rebecca said. "Jewel, will you come, too?"

"For a while." Jewel rose and followed her younger cousins from the drawing room, appearing rather listless.

Cait frowned, wondering if something was bothering her niece. Jewel was usually much more lively.

Everyone else began scattering. Most of the boys trooped upstairs, but Kendra's twins had been conferring. Pol looked to where the girls had disappeared. "We want to hear ghost stories!"

"No boys allowed!" came a voice from the library.

"Not fair," Cas said, looking sulky. Even his blond hair seemed to droop.

"I can tell you a ghost story," Cait offered. "A real one. It happened in Newark-on-Trent—"

"Are you not coming upstairs?" Jason asked.

Crivvens, she had to tell him about the bairn.

She had to. Tonight.

"In a minute," she said, stalling. "Go on up."

THIRTEEN

KENDRA

*B*ACK AT THE cottage, Kendra eyed her chamber suspiciously. "Is there any of that putrid cheese left anywhere?"

"Nowhere." Trick threw the bedcovers back so forcefully they half-landed on the floor. "No mousetraps. No cheese."

She hugged herself. "It's cold in here."

"I can fix that." He strode over to shut the two open windows, then threw another log on the fire, sending sparks flying. "Better?"

"Warmer, for sure." Pomanders had been set about, doubtless by Margaret. Kendra inhaled appreciatively. "It smells lovely in here."

"You smell lovely in here," Trick returned, coming

close enough to overwhelm her senses. His fingers began working the tabs on her stomacher. "At last," he murmured in a husky tone that made her heart skip. "We are *finally* alone—"

A knock on the door interrupted them. Kendra huffed in exasperation.

"Yes?" Trick called irritably, pacing over to open it.

"Good evening, your grace." Margaret entered, steaming tankards in both hands. "I've brought warm ale posset for the two of you."

Looking resigned, he took a tankard and politely sipped from it. "It's delicious. Thank you. You may leave now."

Margaret bustled over to Kendra and handed her the second tankard. "Shall I turn down the bed for you?"

"Thank you, but we've taken care of that." Trick gestured toward the mess he'd made of the bed.

Kendra tasted the posset. "Mmmm. What's in this?"

"Ale and milk and sugar and ginger and nutmeg, and I don't know what else. Some secret ingredient." Margaret leaned close to Kendra to whisper. "The cook here was making some for a friend. She said it stimulates the passions. Given your current troubles, I thought—"

"Please leave now," Trick cut in.

Margaret pretended she hadn't heard him. "Shall I help you undress, your grace?"

"You shall not." Trick began edging her toward the door. "*I* will undress her grace."

Looking scandalized, Margaret hurried out.

After Trick closed the door behind the maid, Kendra released the laugh she'd been holding in. "She said this drink—"

"I heard what she said, and I daresay neither of us needs our passions stimulated. Still and all, I suppose it can't hurt to drink it." Tipping back his head, he drained his tankard in one long draft before slamming it down on the octagonal table.

"Well, then I reckon I'll drink mine, too," Kendra said with a wink. Enjoying Trick's impatient gaze on her, she drank hers down more delicately.

He took the tankard from her hand and slammed it down beside his. "Now…"

Smiling woozily, feeling warm and tingly, she watched him finish detaching her stomacher while her hands went to his laces. Her fingers fumbled. "Od's fish. I'm suddenly feeling very tired. Not pretend-tired so we can get away from everyone, but really, really tired—"

He shut off her words with a kiss. A rush of bliss and excitement overtook her, and she threw her arms around his neck, breathing in his enticing sandalwood scent. But he pulled back all too quickly, blinking in bewilderment. "I'm really tired, too."

"Maybe we should lie down for a few minutes. After the long day, perhaps a tiny nap will revive us."

"Perhaps," he said.

And the next thing she knew, he was on the bed snoring, fully clothed.

A moment after that, she was beside him and sound asleep, too.

FOURTEEN

Caithren

"**W**HERE HAVE you been?" Jason asked Caithren half an hour later. "Surely that tale set in Newark made for a short story. I lived it, if you'll remember, and there wasn't much to it."

He was already in bed.

She'd been half-hoping he'd already be asleep.

Steeling herself to tell him about the bairn, she kicked off her shoes. She'd just answer his question first. "I helped put the children to bed."

"What? They couldn't put themselves to bed?" He set his book on the bedside table. "Jamie is fourteen. And Griffin and Adam—"

"I meant I helped put Kendra's children to bed." She

sat on a chair to roll down her stockings. "Since she and Trick ran off so quickly."

"They aren't little children, either. Elspeth is older than Adam, and Cas and Pol are twelve, aren't they?"

"Thirteen." She rose and began detaching her stomacher. "I just walked them over to the cottage, made sure they didn't need anything, got them some water—"

"And that took forty-five minutes?"

"Well, then I helped pick up all the wrappings and ribbon—"

"Ford has servants to do that."

She shrugged. "I'm sorry. I didn't realize you'd be waiting."

Rising from the bed—stark naked—he moved toward her.

Caithren's breath caught.

"I told you earlier I was missing you. I want you." He reached her in all of two strides. "Surely you don't find that surprising?"

Nay, she didn't find that surprising. The two of them had never tired of each other, never gone more than a handful of days without falling into each other's arms. Nothing had changed that, not children, not familiarity, not time.

She knew the current look in his eyes as well as she knew the back of her own hand. That look made her heart race, as it always did.

She had to tell him she was carrying a bairn.

She had to.

Instead, she stepped into his embrace.

He clasped her tightly against him. His mouth brushed hers, once, twice, caressing her lips more than kissing them, wordlessly commanding her to open and let him in. When she parted her lips, he devoured her mouth with an urgent hunger.

She returned his kiss with wild abandon, stunned at its raw possessiveness. It always felt a wee bit different when they were in a place that wasn't home. A wee bit more exciting. But this was more than that.

What had got into him? Was he still thinking about the journey he was planning for the summer? Was this what he had in mind, day after day of consuming passion? After twenty-one years together, this sounded like a dream. An impossibly beautiful dream.

She had to tell him about the bairn.

But God help her, she didn't want to give up this dream any more than he did.

She had to tell him anyway.

Instead, she helped him rid her of all her remaining clothing.

He crushed her to him, skin against skin, fusing his lips to hers again. His tongue plundered her mouth, his teeth nibbled her lower lip. She wound her arms around his neck and twined her fingers in his long, thick hair, yielding herself to the pleasure. His lips traveled her cheeks, her nose, her hairline. A day's growth of roughness grazed her skin, a thrilling texture even after all their time together, a texture so very, very male.

She had to tell him about the bairn.

Instead, she let him lower her to the bed, his hands roaming her body and leaving a riot of sensation in their wake. Her own hands skimmed his back, his shoulders, wherever she could reach. He smelled spicy and warm, so familiar and yet endlessly, unbearably exciting.

She had to tell him about the bairn.

Instead, she let him kiss her breasts. His dark head bent and his clever mouth moved over them, wet and warm and arousing. In fourteen years, she'd forgotten how sensitive pregnancy made her nipples. Though his teeth grazed her ever so lightly, the resulting sensations straddled the border between exquisite pleasure and enthralling pain. Her bairn-swollen breasts surged in response, sending fiery tendrils throughout her.

She had to tell him about the bairn.

Instead, when his hand traced down her side and his fingers caressed between her legs, she bit her lip to keep from crying out. She pressed her lips to where his neck met his shoulder and tasted his heated skin. His distinctive scent was intoxicating. His low groans echoed her own sounds of bliss, but his movements remained controlled, agonizingly slow, skillfully bringing her to a fever pitch of passion.

She had to tell him about the bairn.

Instead, feeling an incredible urgency, she strained

for more. More of his body, more of his mouth, more of his fingers where they teased. More everywhere. More, more, until there wasn't a spot on her body he hadn't kissed or touched or tantalized into awareness.

She had to tell him about the bairn.

Instead, the sensations built and built, and her pulse raced faster and faster, until she quivered and cried out. And at last he moved over her and slid home.

Welcoming him, wrapping her legs around him, she arched up, taking him deep…deeper…deeper yet, until she felt they were one and the same.

She held her breath while he held still for a beat… two…three.

Then, "Sweet Cait," he murmured, and began rocking against her, slowly at first, then faster, kindling another hot rush of excitement. She met each stroke in exquisite harmony, her entire body pulsing, clutching him with her hands and her legs, with her arms and her heart. Emotions rose within her, overwhelming her body and soul, pushing her up, up…

She was shuddering, gasping for breath. "Oh, no." It was too much. She couldn't stand it.

"Oh, yes," he whispered against her lips. "Fall for me, sweet Cait."

And so she did, plunging over the edge—"Oh, Jase!"—exploding into a million wee pieces when she felt him go with her.

After what seemed an eternity, the pieces slowly

came back together. They lay still for long, satisfying moments before he rolled to his side, taking her with him. She cuddled close as she fought to catch her breath. Gathering her even closer, he graced her with the most tender kiss. A kiss that melted her heart, her lips clinging to his, savoring the sweetness of his love, a love that had never faltered.

She had to tell him about the bairn.

She'd tell him after Christmas.

That was only two days from now, after all.

What harm could come from waiting?

FIFTEEN

COLIN

ON CHRISTMAS Eve morning, Colin grabbed a mug of coffee from the kitchen and headed to the side door that led to the courtyard and the cottage. He opened it to find Jewel on the other side, about to enter.

Both of them startled, then laughed. He went past her and outdoors.

She turned to face him. "Papa, are you leaving?" she asked incredulously. "Breakfast starts at nine. Which is now."

"You know I never eat breakfast." He raised the mug of coffee. "This is all I want. I'm off to take a bath."

Beyond the open door, Elspeth, Diana, and Rebecca

could be seen making their way to the dining room from their sleeping quarters in the library.

"The whole family will be at breakfast!" Jewel protested, gesturing toward the girls. "You don't have to eat. You can just sit and drink your coffee and talk."

"We have three days together," he said reasonably. "A single breakfast isn't that important."

Seven assorted sons and nephews clattered down the stairs.

Jewel frowned at him. "Mama will think that's rude."

"I've already told her what I'm doing, and she doesn't seem to mind. I'm looking forward to some peace in my chamber. I'll catch up with everyone after you've eaten," he added and headed for the cottage.

Or at least he hoped Jewel *thought* he'd headed to the cottage.

Instead, once she'd closed the side door, he went around the house to the front door and into the entrance hall. There, he sipped the coffee while covertly watching everyone else make their way to breakfast.

Violet and Ford came downstairs next. Kendra's twins came in through the side door, Amy trailing in after them. The noise level rose in the rapidly filling dining room as Cait and Jason came down and joined everyone at the table.

He lingered a while longer, waiting to see if Kendra and Trick would show up. When minutes passed and they didn't, he chuckled to himself, returned the empty mug to the kitchen, and headed up the stairs.

Which was how he managed to get to Ford's top-floor laboratory undetected. But the door was locked. Again.

With a sigh, he parked himself in the corridor until a young housemaid came along.

"Can I help you, my lord?"

"I was hoping to get into Lord Lakefield's laboratory. But it's locked."

"He often keeps it locked, especially when there are guests in the house. He claims things in there are dangerous. We're not even allowed to clean it." She eyed him speculatively. "Are you wanting something in the laboratory?"

"I was hoping I might find a tool or two, so I can fix a loose hinge in my room. I think what I need is pliers. Very strong pliers," he added under his breath.

"Oh, you'll find tools in the household office, my lord. I have a key for that." She beckoned him to follow her. "Right over here—" She stopped and turned. "Although surely you'd rather have a footman fix it?"

"Surely they're all busy serving breakfast? I don't mind fixing it myself," he assured her, then flashed her a disarming smile.

He watched a blush creep into her cheeks and congratulated himself as she let him into the office.

After all these years, he could still dazzle an unsuspecting girl.

If only he were still able to dazzle his wife.

Fixing his marriage was much more important than fixing anything in the cottage—or *un*fixing something in the cottage, which was what he was actually planning.

His prank was progressing brilliantly, which was fun.

However, he was rapidly discovering it wasn't fun enough to offset the mounting trouble in his life.

He had yet to figure out what was making Jewel so dispirited. Hugh still wanted to go off to war. And though he'd been wracking his brain for what felt like forever, he couldn't find a way to make things right for both Amy and Aidan.

Long ago, he'd once had to choose between Amy and his estate. Did he now have to choose between Amy and his son? Or was the choice between his son and his honor?

He found himself on the horns of a dilemma. Which was the lesser evil? Or could there possibly be another way?

He was beginning to think not. And if there was no way out, he could see only one way through.

SIXTEEN

KENDRA

"*Y*OUR GRACE?"

Kendra rolled over to find the bedroom door cracked open. "Hmm, Margaret?"

"Your family is waiting for you for breakfast. Do you want me to tell them that you and his grace would rather sleep?"

Although a slit in the curtains revealed that it was light outdoors, it felt like the middle of the night. Kendra tried to blink herself awake. "What time is it?"

"Half past nine in the morning, your grace."

Half past nine in the morning? Kendra usually rose by eight.

She struggled up on her elbows and noticed she

wasn't under the covers. She peeked over the edge of the bed to find the covers were on the floor.

And she was dressed. When had she dressed? She turned to see Trick. He was snoozing away and dressed as well.

In last night's clothes.

And her gown was the one she'd worn last night.

The open door blocked Margaret's view of them, for which she was thankful. "What's happening?" she called toward the entrance, thoroughly confused.

"It's half past nine, your grace. And your family is waiting for breakfast."

"Oh, yes, you said that already. My apologies—I fear I was half asleep. Let me just wake his grace. Tell the family we'll be there as soon as possible, and they are welcome to begin without us."

As Margaret closed the door, Kendra rolled over.

"Trick." She jogged his shoulder. "Trick!"

"Hmm?"

"It's half past nine! We must change and get to breakfast!"

His amber eyes lazily opened, then quickly shut. "Too tired."

She still felt quite tired as well. "How on earth did this happen?" She jogged his shoulder another time, none too gently, then forced herself to rise and begin pulling her gown off. "We have to change. The family is waiting on us for breakfast, and we cannot show up in yesterday's clothes."

Slowly Trick sat up and rubbed his eyes, then looked down at his gray breeches. "We overslept? In our clothes?"

"Evidence would suggest that." She crossed to the wardrobe to pull out a fresh gown. "And we failed to make love."

"Well then, come over here—"

"Trr-rick! They're waiting!"

It was tempting—sorely tempting—but that simply wouldn't be decent. Not while family was seated around the table, expecting them to arrive. Besides, they'd tried that yesterday, while their children were waiting for breakfast, to no avail. She liked to think she could learn from her mistakes.

"Get up," she demanded fiercely.

"Hearts wounds," he said with a groan. "Give a man a minute."

"I'll give you two. And then we'll come back here straight after we eat," she added, her lips curving in a suggestive smile. "I promise."

"Very well," he muttered, pushing himself to stand. "But only because a Chase promise is not given lightly. And never broken, aye?" He met her gaze, his hot. "I'll be holding you to that."

SEVENTEEN

JEWEL

*A*UNTY KENDRA stabbed a bite of her eggs. "Why isn't Colin here?"

"He never eats breakfast," Jewel told her and sipped her tea.

"But this is a family occasion." Aunty Cait looked to Mama. "Don't you think that's ill-mannered?"

"He's not quite himself these days, and he truly doesn't eat breakfast. He just takes a cup of coffee to his study." Mama shrugged. "He told me he wanted a bath, and I decided not to argue."

"He told me that, too," Jewel said.

Privately, she wondered if he were actually avoiding her mother. Mama certainly didn't seem to mind. She wished the two of them would settle the issue with

120 | LAUREN ROYAL

Aidan one way or another, so her life could get back to normal.

Or at least as normal as life could be, considering she was contemplating an immense, life-altering decision.

"Colin won't skip breakfast tomorrow," Violet predicted. "Not when we'll be serving my family's traditional Christmas breakfast."

"What will we be having?" Cas asked at the same time Pol asked, "What is your family's Christmas breakfast?"

"Your sons are such typical Chase males," Mama told Aunty Kendra. "Asking about the next meal while eating this one."

Violet laughed. "My mother has always served panperdy, buttered eggs with bacon, hot pan cakes with butter and sugar—"

"And warmed chocolate!" the twins' sister Diana interrupted. "How is it that neither of you remember?"

"Your brothers were but nine the last time we had Christmas here," Aunty Kendra reminded her. "Four years is a long time when you're thirteen."

"Indeed," Uncle Ford put in, "that's nearly thirty-one percent of their lives to date."

Trust Uncle Ford to calculate everything, Jewel thought while the rest of the family ignored his comment. She swallowed her last bite. "May I be excused? I need to finish wrapping my gifts."

"But we're going to skate!" her cousin Adam protested. "With our new skates! Remember?"

"That's right." She'd been so distracted by Henry's proposal that she'd completely forgotten. "I suppose I'll wrap them later."

Aunty Kendra cleared her throat. "We need to wrap our gifts too, and I'd rather do that now and skate later."

"Your gifts are already wrapped," Diana declared with a frown. "I saw them."

"You cannot have seen all of them," her father said firmly. "Because we still have some to wrap. In our chamber."

Jewel looked between Aunty Kendra and Uncle Trick. They both seemed much too determined to wrap gifts.

In their chamber.

What was going on?

"I'm nearly done implementing a new idea in my laboratory," Uncle Ford said, "and I've a hankering to finish. How about if we each attend to our own tasks until dinner, then we'll all skate afterwards?"

"Sounds good," Uncle Trick said at the same time his four children shouted, "No!"

"I want to skate now!"

"We just ate!"

"Dinner won't be for hours!"

"I don't want to wait!"

Twelve cousins registered twelve different protests, all at once.

"The weather will be warmer after dinner," Aunty Violet proclaimed as though that decided everything. Which Jewel supposed was the case, since Violet was in charge. "We'll eat at noon, and then we'll skate afterwards."

"Noon isn't even two hours from now," her eldest, Nicolas, pointed out. "Our breakfast was too late. We ought to skip dinner."

"We are not skipping anything," Violet said, looking no less determined. "Not after Hilda went to so much trouble procuring supplies and making plans. So we'll eat light, which is best before skating anyway."

"And also because we need to save room for our big Christmas Eve supper tonight," Aunty Cait put in. "With plum pudding." She rubbed her hands together. "Kendra, you must be looking forward to plum pudding."

Jewel looked to see what Aunty Kendra had to say to that, but she and Uncle Trick had apparently slipped from the room when she wasn't watching.

To go wrap gifts?

Somehow, she thought not.

First Papa skipped out on breakfast, and now Aunty Kendra and Uncle Trick had vanished as well. Were the two disappearances connected?

A very interesting puzzle.

EIGHTEEN

KENDRA

"*H*URRY," KENDRA said as she and Trick rushed up the cottage's staircase. "I intend to be in bed with you before anyone else steps foot in this building."

"Sounds good to me," he said, sidling past her to hurry down the corridor. He reached for the door latch.

BANG!

Kendra stopped so abruptly she nearly ran into him.

"Sweet Mary!" he breathed.

They both stared at their bedchamber's door.

Which was flat on their bedchamber's floor.

Trick blinked, looking bewildered. "What the devil happened to the pins that go in the hinges?"

"I cannot imagine." Kendra felt as if all the air had

quite suddenly been sucked out of her. "They're just... gone." She looked up at him quizzically. "How can they have disappeared?"

Trick went inside, stepping on the fallen door and pulling her in after him. "I don't know, and right now I don't care." He lifted the door and set it back in place, carefully aligning the empty knuckles of the hinges. "It matters not," he said, moving her toward the bed, a lascivious gleam in his eyes. "We cannot allow"—a knock came at the door, immediately followed by another—

BANG!

"Your grace?" Margaret stepped onto the floored-again door, looking bemused. "My apologies, your graces. I heard a loud noise, and came to—"

"We could have been standing there!" Kendra cried. "Right where that door fell! You could have killed us!"

"She didn't," Trick told her succinctly before turning to Margaret. "What the devil happened to the pins that go in the hinges?"

"The pins?" She looked to the doorframe, then down to the edge of the door. "Lud. I—I don't know."

"Well, go find out, will you?" His huff was half apology, half exasperation. "That is, *please* go find out. We'll wait here—out of the range of this damned door."

"Come back with pins!" Kendra yelled after her.

NINETEEN

JEWEL

*I*N HER LITTLE private bedchamber, as she folded fabric around her last gift, Jewel was still mentally debating whether she should marry Henry. Last night, she'd been doubting he really loved her. But the truth was, she wasn't any more certain that *she* loved *him*.

And she wondered if that really mattered.

As a small girl, she'd dreamed of true, everlasting love—how could she not, having grown up with her parents, aunts, and uncles as examples? That dream hadn't died, but she was old enough now to have noticed such love was rare. And she liked to think she was sensible. Didn't it make sense to choose a pleasant life over a lonely one, given that an exceedingly passionate life was unlikely?

She'd turned down countless suitors, waiting for the right one, until Henry walked into her life. Surely by now she'd met every eligible young man in the kingdom—the aristocracy comprised a small social circle, after all. At this point, anyone she hadn't met probably lived in the north, which was entirely too far from her family.

Could she do better than Henry?

She thought not.

Although she wasn't sure she loved Henry, she was very sure she *liked* him. He was good and decent. He would make a kind husband and father. And she wanted children. Perhaps she should say yes. Maybe it would be best to get herself a husband and get on with her life, put the tiresome matchmaking-go-round behind her.

She envisioned herself in the big workshop Henry had said he'd build for her. In her mental picture, she was creating an exquisite stained-glass window, a dark-haired little girl and a tow-headed little boy by her side, both of them learning her craft.

Smiling, she tied the final ribbon. Then she rose and stretched and left the room. Thinking it felt good to be closer to a decision, she turned to head down the stairs.

Just then, a shriek came from the far end of the corridor. Alarmed, she turned back to investigate.

The door that led to Aunty Kendra and Uncle Trick's chamber was open. Or at least it *looked* open, until she got closer and saw it was not strictly open, but rather completely disconnected and propped against the wall.

How on earth did *that* happen?

Something was going on, Jewel thought, remembering her aunt and uncle's odd behavior at breakfast.

A discussion was wafting from the room, just garbled enough that she couldn't make out the words. She frowned and moved yet closer.

"One of the pins fell out of its hinge," a female voice said, "and—"

"How on earth did *that* happen?" Uncle Trick interrupted, echoing Jewel's thoughts in a much more annoyed tone. "It should have been wedged in there so tight—"

"Apparently it was broken, your grace. They had to take the other pin to the blacksmith, so he could make a match. I'm so sorry," the female added in a soothing manner. "Mr. Harry assured me it would be fixed by tonight."

"Tonight? *Tonight?* I want to scream!" Aunty Kendra all but screamed.

Something was going on—Jewel was sure of it now. Her aunt and uncle were clearly desperate to be alone in their chamber, and she could think of just one thing married couples did alone in their chamber. Something was preventing them…

Quite definitely, something was going on.

Something devious.

And in the Chase family sphere, something devious usually meant something cooked up by Papa.

She felt close to putting the pieces together when she heard Uncle Trick say, "You may leave, and please don't return until we call for you."

Hearing footsteps approach the doorway, Jewel rushed to the other end of the corridor.

A young maid exited the room, looking like she was stifling a giggle.

Very curious. Or…

Perhaps not curious at all.

In fact, it made perfect sense.

Jewel approached her at a measured pace, contriving a meeting point out of hearing range from her aunt and uncle's bedchamber. When the girl moved aside to allow her to pass, her gaze lowered deferentially, Jewel turned and tapped her on the shoulder. "Pardon me," she said quietly. "Are you the duchess's maid?"

The maid gasped and whirled, both hands to her heart, making Jewel wonder why she should be so skittish. Then she blinked a few times and relaxed, apparently finding a woman close to her age less frightening than expected. Her gaze flicked to the room she'd just left, then back to Jewel.

"Yes," she said in a whisper. "I'm Margaret."

Hoping to set her at ease, Jewel smiled. "May I speak with you in my chamber?"

The maid hesitantly nodded, then followed her down the corridor and into her room.

Jewel shut the door and waved her over to a chair, taking the chair across the small table for herself. "Will you tell me what's going on?"

Perched at the very edge of the chair with her hands folded in her lap, Margaret gazed at her innocently. "I don't understand. Nothing is going on. Nothing unusual, I mean. Why do you ask, my lady?"

"Because I have eyes in my head, and a working set of ears as well. Plus a quick mind, or so I'm told. I've been observing you"—Jewel watched the maid's eyes widen—"and I believe you and my father are playing a masterful prank." She paused for a breath. "And I want in on it."

The girl's eyes widened further before a reluctant little laugh burst out of her. "You do?"

"Of course I do. There's nothing quite so fun as a good prank." Not to mention it would be something to occupy her mind besides Henry. She hadn't felt like herself since he'd proposed—a piece of mischief might be just the thing to revive her old spirit. "Are you keeping my aunt and uncle, um...apart?"

Margaret blushed. "Yes. Yes, we are. I mean, your father is keeping them apart, with my help." She looked away. "I know it's terrible of me to play a prank on my mistress, especially her grace, who's so very kind, but—"

"My father bribed you, didn't he?"

That startled another laugh out of Margaret. "How did you know?"

"I know my father," Jewel said with a rueful shake of her head. "Of course he bribed you. He always finds a way to get what he wants." Well, not with her mother lately, not yet, but he would, Jewel was sure of it. "How much has he promised you?"

"Twenty pounds. I'm not proud of it." Margaret's eyes glazed with a thin sheen of unshed tears, horrifying Jewel. She hadn't meant to upset Aunt Kendra's maid—she'd just wanted to hear about the prank. "I said no to five and no to ten," Margaret elaborated in a tiny voice, "but then he offered twenty, and…do you think I'm an awful person?"

"Not at all," Jewel said gently. "Twenty pounds is nothing to my father. And I have a feeling you must want that money for a very good reason."

"Not good enough," the maid said with a little sniffle. "My reason is selfish. I should never have agreed."

Margaret seemed so sweet and earnest, Jewel couldn't help but like her. And feel for her. "Tell me." Jewel pulled a handkerchief out of her sleeve and handed it to her. "Tell me your reason. I'd wager it's not selfish at all."

"It *is* selfish." Margaret dabbed at her eyes and nose.

"I want to get married, and I don't want to wait three years."

"Are you in love?" Jewel asked, feeling a little stab of jealousy when Margaret nodded.

Jewel was probably a year or two older than Margaret, yet she wasn't sure she'd ever been in love. Once she'd *thought* she was in love, but she'd been all of ten then, and she'd been wrong. Eleven years had allowed her to put things in perspective.

She'd known Henry but a few weeks, yet she was already certain he was the best of all the young men who had courted her. Perhaps that meant she was falling in love with him. Or maybe she was already in love. How was one supposed to know when one was in love, anyway? She didn't know how to tell.

"Yes, I'm very much in love," Margaret said as though the nod hadn't been confirmation enough. Or maybe she just wanted to say it out loud.

"Then why should you have to wait three years?" Jewel asked, pushing the envy away. "Whom are you in love with? Start with that."

Margaret tucked an errant strand of russet hair back under her cap. "His name is Richard Turner. He's a footman at Foxbow Manor, an estate that borders Amberley."

Amberley belonged to Uncle Trick, which meant Margaret lived there, near her beau. "A footman sounds like a reasonable match for you," Jewel said. "Surely you're not too young." Margaret appeared to be eighteen at least. "And I assume he's not too young to wed, either. I've no doubt my uncle would be willing to employ him so the two of you can live together—my uncle is as kind as my aunt."

"I know," Margaret said. "It's thanks to your uncle that I was raised in a lovely home and fed and educated. I know his grace would employ Richard if we asked. Well, maybe he wouldn't…"

"Why would you say that?"

"Oh, her grace seems to think I should find employment elsewhere. I think she wants to train someone new from the orphanage." The maid sighed. "Regardless, that isn't why Richard and I cannot marry anytime soon."

Jewel absently shuffled her gaily wrapped packages on the table. "Then why should you have to wait?"

Hesitation narrowed Margaret's blue eyes, and then, "We lost a silver tray," she rushed out. "I've not told anyone this, but the two of us lost a large silver tray last summer. Lady Foxbow had ordered it specially made, and it cost thirty-four pounds, and Richard was tasked to fetch it from the village. I had a half day off, so I went with him—we walked to the village together, so happy and carefree. The tray was wrapped in brown paper tied with string, and we were thirsty after the long walk, so we carried it to a taproom and set it down and drank some ale. When we got up to leave, it was gone. Just gone."

Jewel had never seen anyone look quite so wan. Simply gazing at Margaret made her heart hurt. "That's very unfortunate, but why should it keep you from wedding?"

"The tray cost thirty-four pounds, my lady. Thirty-four pounds! Richard earns five pounds a year and I earn another five—in the time since we lost the tray, he's been able to pay just four pounds towards that debt. Even should we both save every penny, it will take him three more years to clear the debt, and Lord Foxbow won't free him to hire on elsewhere before the debt is paid."

"That's rather harsh." Jewel shook her head. "Well, perhaps you can find employment on the Foxbow estate instead?"

"I'm loath to leave her grace, but that doesn't signify, because Lord Foxbow does not allow his servants to wed."

"Lord Foxbow sounds dreadful," Jewel said darkly.

Margaret just shrugged. "Surely you know rules like these are common."

"Yes, I know," Jewel said with a sigh. "I do know that."

None of the Chases forbade their servants to marry, but plenty of other families did. And it certainly wasn't uncommon for employers to demand payment for lost or broken items, although Jewel couldn't imagine her parents doing that, either.

She did some quick math in her head. "Twenty pounds will allow you to marry two years sooner."

Margaret nodded soberly. "That's why I agreed to help, even though I knew it was wrong."

"I understand," Jewel assured her. "And I don't blame you for agreeing at all. A wait of one year will be much more tolerable than three."

Needless to say, a wait of no years at all would be more tolerable still—and Jewel believed she could achieve that end. But she felt she ought not to raise her new friend's hopes until all was in place.

And in the meantime, she and Margaret would have some fun.

TWENTY

Kendra

*A*T LONG LAST, Kendra and Trick were on the bed. They were *in* the bed. After wasting much too much time being frustrated, they'd propped the door back in place and moved the heavy washstand against it. Their mouths were fused together, and Trick's hands were going everywhere, and Kendra's heart was racing, and everything felt heavenly—

Scccrrrape...

BANG!

Kendra wrenched her lips from Trick's. "Do not *dare* come in here!" she hollered, rolling over to see the door on the floor again—and the washstand halfway into the room.

"Are you ready for dinner?" Cas called.

Or maybe that was Pol. She never could tell the two of them apart when she could only hear but not see them.

Trick's hands on her had stilled. Mostly. "Hush," he whispered. "Maybe they'll leave us alone."

"We're not going to leave you alone," Cas or Pol said. "Everyone is waiting for you for dinner. Make haste—we want to skate!"

Kendra rolled away from her husband and plunked a pillow over her face.

Trick made a curious noise. "What are you doing?"

In answer, she simply screamed.

TWENTY-ONE

JEWEL

*D*INNER WAS A short, hurried affair, as no
one was terribly hungry and the cousins
were anxious to go skating. Aunty Kendra and Uncle
Trick were both irritable, amusing Jewel to the point
where she hardly thought about marrying Henry at all.

But afterward, back in her chamber, she did think
about him while she pulled on her warmest clothes. She
couldn't seem to help herself—her life seemed reduced
to making this decision. She felt so close.

Why couldn't she just commit? What was she
waiting for?

With a sigh, she grabbed her new skates and headed
out of the room. Or rather, she opened the door,

intending to head out of the room, but found Margaret there waiting.

The maid beckoned her back inside. "Are you in a rush, my lady?" she asked quietly. "I'm wondering if you could help me with something. I don't think it should make you too late for the skating."

It had to be something to do with the prank. Jewel smiled. "Of course," she said, beginning to remove her cloak.

"No, my lady, you'll want to keep that on." Margaret's eyes danced conspiratorially, making Jewel like her even more. "We're heading to the stables."

"Oh!" Jewel shrugged back into the garment. "This sounds like fun. By the by, may I ask you for a favor?"

Margaret looked puzzled. "Anything, my lady. Anything at all."

"I'd like to keep my involvement in this a secret from my father for now."

The maid's eyes widened. "I'll not say anything, unless he asks me directly—"

"He won't," Jewel assured her with a grin. "Shall we go?"

TWENTY-TWO

KENDRA

"$\mathcal{T}$he skates are working brilliantly Uncle Ford!" Kendra's eldest, Elspeth, called while gracefully gliding on one foot with her other leg raised in the air.

Laughter rang out over the icy pond. The younger girls were competing to see which of them could twirl the longest, judged by Jewel, who had joined their skating party a little late. Most of the boys were skating races.

When Chases were involved, it seemed everything was a contest, but Kendra wouldn't want it any other way. It was nice to see her children enjoying themselves in the midst of her personal frustrations.

But, oh, were those personal frustrations frustrating.

She could scarcely believe she and Trick still hadn't managed to get together. She felt like powder keg about to explode, her skin tight and hot, her stomach constantly tied in knots. While all around her, everyone else was blithely enjoying the holiday.

Well, maybe not everyone…

She skated over to Amy, matching strokes to glide side-by-side. "I know why you're unhappy, but why is Jewel in the doldrums? She's usually so spirited."

"I wish I knew," Amy said with a sigh. "Colin thinks it's because she lost her maid, but I fear it's something more. Something she's not sharing."

"Perhaps she's worried about the invasion."

"Perhaps." Amy shook her head, looking troubled. "Aren't we all?"

Kendra could only nod her agreement.

England's last civil war had taken so much from her: her parents, her home, her childhood. She couldn't bear to think of it all happening again. More families torn apart, more bloodshed and destruction…

It was a welcome distraction when Ford *whooshed* past them, skating backward as he called out, "Watch this!" While everyone turned to look, he lifted his heels and came to a gentle halt, making a scraping noise in the process.

Kendra gasped. "How'd you *do* that?"

He laughed and skated closer, tracing circles around her. "While you were wrapping your gifts, I was carving jagged teeth into the front of my blades." He sounded very pleased with himself. "I thought they would make a good stopping mechanism. Do you want to see it again?"

Kendra nodded eagerly.

While she watched, he turned to skate backward in a big circle, doing the crossover strokes that she and her siblings had learned long ago in the Netherlands during the Commonwealth years. Which she didn't find particularly impressive, given that she was a competent skater herself. But then he seemed to reach a slippery patch of ice and lose his balance, his arms windmilling to keep him upright.

Kendra laughed as he hurtled past her. "Very impressive!" she teased.

He gave her a sour look, which became a look of shock as he hit an uneven patch. Some instinct made him swiftly turn forward and jam the front of one skate into the ice, evidently trying to stop, but instead it had the curious effect of launching him into the air. As the entire family watched in amazement, Ford spun halfway round in the air and landed on the opposite leg, skating backward again.

"Uncle Ford!" Adam cried. "How did you do *that?*"

"I want teeth on the front of *my* blades!" young Rebecca called out.

When Ford came to a stop, half the children converged on him, demanding that he teach them.

"What the devil *was* that?" Jason wondered.

"I don't know," Ford said in a daze, oblivious to the children hanging all over him. "But I bet I can work out how to do it again…"

He began muttering under his breath, his gaze trained on the ice.

Kendra rolled her eyes, knowing her twin would now stay up half the night employing complicated physics equations to learn how to skate-jump on purpose. Not that she wasn't as thrilled as the rest of her family. In fact, of all the remarkable things Ford had invented, these ingenious new skate blades might be her favorite.

Jason skated up to her. "It's nice to see you smiling. Happy, Kendra?"

"About some things," she said ruefully.

"About most things, I'm hoping." He grabbed her to skate arm-in-arm, as he had when she was a child and had needed him to hold her up. "Careful, now," he said as he had way back then, mentally sending her back to a frozen canal in Holland, where they had been exiled along with King Charles. "Remember to push out to the side."

She laughed. "I remember. How about you?"

"How about what?"

"Are you happy, too? How do you feel about the babe?"

"The babe?"

"The..." Her feet stopped pushing sideways—stopped moving at all. At the edge of the ice, far from the rest of the family, she skidded to a stop. "The baby. Cait told you, surely? She promised she would."

His hands on her shoulders, he turned her to face him. "The baby?"

"She didn't? Oh, my God, I'm—"

"I'm feeling stupid," he interrupted. "What baby, Kendra? What on earth are you talking about?"

"Cait's. And yours, of course. She's..." She searched his eyes, seeing only confusion. "Cait's with child," she finished as gently as she could. "I thought she'd told you."

"She told you before me?" He'd gone white, the freckles he'd inherited from their mother suddenly visible on his pale face. "Who else knows?"

"Only Amy and Violet. Cait was afraid to tell you, afraid to ruin your happiness. But she promised us she would. Oh, Jason, I'm so sorry. I—"

He wasn't listening. While she was rattling on, he was tramping through the snow toward a stand of trees, his skates still attached to his boots.

She looked around, but no one else had noticed. Ford and Violet were skating together, lost in conversation, and the youngsters had gone back to what they were doing before his demonstration. Cait and Amy were now judging the girls' twirling competition, since Jewel and Elspeth had decided to join in, and Trick and Colin were timing the boys with one of Ford's newfangled watches. All the cousins were having the time of their lives.

In the meantime, Jason had disappeared from view, gone who knows where.

What had she done?

"Jase?" she heard Cait call. "Jason?" She was looking all around. "Where's Jason?"

Kendra skated over to her. "He left."

"He left? Where did he go?"

"Back to the house, I'm thinking." Kendra pulled her farther away from the others. "Cait...I asked him how he felt about the baby."

Cait went even whiter than Jason had. "What?"

"I thought you'd told him about it, and—"

"Three men can keep a secret if twa are deed," Cait interrupted.

It was Kendra's turn to say "What?"

"One of Mam's old sayings. There is no such thing as a secret. Crivvens." She drew a deep breath and blew it out, a visible puff in the cold air. "I don't blame you— this is my fault. Was he angry?"

"I don't know. He just...walked off. On his skates."

"Well, then, he cannot have got far." Pulling a key from her pocket, Cait sat right there on the ice to unlatch her own skates. "I'll just go after him."

TWENTY-THREE

CAITHREN

*W*HEN EVERYONE was chilled to the bone, they returned to the house where Caithren was waiting.

Without Jason.

They all looked happy as they trooped in, cheeks flushed with cold and fun, chattering and teasing one another—the exact opposite of Cait's current mood. It struck her as unfair that they felt so jolly while she felt so miserable, although she knew that made her a crabbit human being.

"Children!" Violet chided not a moment after the door was shut. "Your cloaks and skates belong in your rooms, not on the floor in here."

The young ones scattered, the lads heading upstairs, the lasses to their temporary library-bedroom.

After hanging her own cloak on one of the pegs Ford had put on the wall for that purpose, Kendra looked to Cait. "Is Jason upstairs?"

"No." Cait hugged herself, feeling cold even near the roaring fire. "He's not here. I cannot imagine where he's gone. He must be terribly upset."

"I'm sure he was just surprised," Kendra said in a tone clearly meant to be soothing.

But Cait didn't feel soothed, especially when she realized that everyone—or all of the adults, at least—now knew that Jason had gone missing. And, given the way they were shooting her concerned looks, they doubtless also knew the rest: that she was carrying a bairn and had failed to tell him.

Wheesht! Was there no privacy in this family?

Well, of course there wasn't, she chided herself. Hadn't she said there was no such thing as a secret? A mere hour ago, no less?

"Have you looked in the cottage?" Amy asked gently.

"Aye," Cait admitted, "which was silly, considering we're not staying there. I've looked everywhere. Except the laboratory."

"It's locked," Ford told her.

"Which was why I didn't look."

"He won't be in there, but I'll go look anyway," he said and ran up the stairs.

"Your grace?" Lakefield's houseman, Harry, stepped into the room and went to Kendra. "Your maid asked me to tell you your door has been repaired."

"Excellent!" she said so brightly that Cait wanted to slap her.

Violet also summoned cheer from out of thin air. "Shall we sing more carols while we wait for Jason?"

"I don't feel like singing," Cait said with a decisive shake of her head.

"I'm sure Jason will appear soon, and then you'll want to sing." Amy came closer to give her a quick hug. "Did you check the stables?"

"Why would he hide there?" Colin asked. "It's freezing in the stables."

"Yes, it is," Rebecca piped up indignantly as she returned, still wearing her cloak. "I'm going to check on my poor kitties."

As the side door blew closed behind Rebecca, Ford returned. "Jason wasn't in the laboratory. But I'm sure he's fine—he'll show up when he's ready."

"I hope so," Cait said bleakly.

She really should have told him about the bairn. But she'd known this news would make him unhappy, and her fears had come true. And—as everyone had warned her—keeping the secret had only made things worse. Now she had to wonder whether he was more upset about the babe or the fact that she'd hidden her pregnancy from him. Again.

Would he ever forgive her?

Oh, very well, she knew that he would.

Eventually.

But even so, she feared he would feel resentful and discontented for the next few years, until the bairn was no longer a needy babe and they could live the life he'd been picturing.

And that would be awful.

And if he didn't want this child, would he be able to love it the same way he loved Griffin, Adam, and Jamie?

She placed her hands on her middle, fighting back tears at the mere thought of the child within her facing life without the comfort of a loving father.

"Cait, he'll be back," Violet stated bluntly. "I think we should sing." She gestured toward the harpsichord. "Kendra?"

"It will be a while before all the children reassemble." Exchanging a glance with Trick, Kendra drew her cloak off the peg she'd so recently left it on. "I'd like to change out of these hot clothes."

"Me, too," Trick said. He hadn't bothered taking his cloak off. "I'll go with you."

The two of them began inching toward the lobby.

"I think we should all change," Colin suggested. "This outdoor clothing *is* too warm, and evening is approaching quickly." He looked to Cait. "Perhaps we should ready ourselves for Christmas Eve supper and *then* sing more carols?"

Cait just shrugged. She couldn't find the energy for more of a response.

"Changing sounds good," Violet agreed in much too merry a tone. "Shall we meet back here in, say, twenty minutes?"

"I brought a very elaborate new dress, so I expect I'll take longer than twenty minutes," Kendra called from the door to the courtyard. As she and Trick walked out, she raised her voice to a level that would best be described as a shout. "But Elspeth knows most of the carols, so she can play until I return!"

Cait sighed, imagining herself smothered in exuberant caroling.

The joy of Christmas.

TWENTY-FOUR

Kendra

*T*RICK AND Kendra were walking so fast they made it nearly to the cottage before anyone else even emerged from the house. "What are the odds they'll believe we're just changing?" he asked.

"Zero." She linked her arm in his, feeling more light-hearted than she had in days. "What are the odds I care?"

"Zero as well?" Laughing, he pulled her inside the building, slammed the door, and pushed her back against it, fusing his mouth to hers.

For a heady minute, she lost herself in his embrace, a warm glow spreading through her. But eventually she had to come up for air. "Um, there are servants in here.

And Cas or Pol could walk in. Or Jewel, or Amy and Colin—"

"I hear you. Let's go up."

Kendra struggled out of her cloak as they raced to the bedroom door, which thankfully was back in place. She opened it and stepped inside.

And dropped the cloak.

And sneezed.

"No." The word was a groan. Her eyes were watering already. "I cannot believe this!"

Cats were everywhere, wandering the floor and perched on the furniture. Three of the dratted things were snoozing cozily on the bed, as though the room weren't bitterly cold. A tabby wandered up and poked beneath her skirts.

"Shoo, cat, shoo!" Shivering and sneezing at the same time, she fought back tears of frustration. "Oh, my God, Trick, what next?"

"Go downstairs," he said. "I'll find Margaret and see that she gets rid of the creatures."

"Make sure she shuts the windows, too. We could freeze to death in here. And tell her to brush this." She snatched up her cloak and shoved it at him. "It's probably covered in cat hair already. I'll wait in the common room."

As she went down the stairs, Colin and Amy were coming up. "Are you all right, Kendra?" Amy asked. "You look upset."

"There are cats in my chamber. Cats!"

Colin eyes widened. "How on earth did *that* happen?"

"A mystery for the ages," she muttered, moving past them and swiping at her damp eyes.

Why did terrible things keep happening? And how had she let herself lose her temper with Trick? She shouldn't be shoving things at him—her cloak or anything else. None of this was his fault. She hardly recognized the woman she was becoming.

"Would you like to switch chambers with us?" Amy called from above.

Kendra stopped to look up. "Oh. Yes. I appreciate the idea and the offer." A small measure of relief trickled through her as she added, "You have my thanks—this will be much more prudent than hoping my room might be cleaned well enough. I'll ask Margaret to move our things while we're at supper."

"And we'll ask Benchley," Amy replied before continuing upstairs.

The room swap would mean she'd sleep better, Kendra thought as she tromped down to the ground floor, but it didn't solve her more pressing predicament: her unprecedented, unquenched longing.

Exasperated, she dropped to one of the plush couches in the common room. A moment later, she rose and fetched a blanket to wrap around her shivering shoulders. She sat again. She rose again to move to the couch nearest the fire.

The main door opened. Cas and Pol meandered in and headed toward their room, then stopped when they saw her.

Pol's brows knitted in concern. "Why are you still wearing that dress, Mama?"

"There are cats in my chamber. Cats!"

"Oh." Cas grimaced before he sneezed—in sympathy, apparently, since she wasn't reacting to any cats down here. "That's awful."

"Go change into your Christmas Eve clothing," she told them. "You won't want to miss the caroling."

They left her alone to brood. She watched for her niece to come in, so she could complain to her, too. But Jewel was taking her blessed time. Or maybe she was upstairs already.

A few minutes later Trick found her, Margaret in tow.

The maid's blue eyes were glassy with remorse, her hands clasped together tightly. "My apologies, your grace."

"Why on earth were the windows open?"

"I...I was tidying and thought I could still smell some cheese. I opened the windows to air out the room. I didn't think cats would get in. Weren't they supposed to be locked in the stables?"

"Maybe Rebecca let them out." Kendra looked to Trick. "Or Jason, if he went in there."

Margaret shook her head. "Regardless, your grace, your room is upstairs. Upstairs, so high! I never considered—"

"There's a tree branch not a foot from one of those windows," Trick pointed out kindly.

"I'm so sorry!" Now Margaret looked panicked. "Please don't send me away to live with strangers!"

"I'm not going to send you away," Kendra said with a sigh, wishing she'd never mentioned the possibility before she'd had a new position secured. In the face of Margaret's fears, she felt the anger seeping out of her.

If only the lust were waning as well.

She sighed again. "We'll be moving to the chamber next door, so please cooperate with Lord Greystone's valet. Oh, and bring me the gown I chose for supper, so I can change in the twins' room once they're ready. With any luck, this will be the last of our troubles."

Not that luck had been in her favor lately.

TWENTY-FIVE

Amy

BAREFOOT, AMY padded across the room to open the wardrobe cabinet.

"Poor Kendra," she mused as she pulled out the deep amethyst gown she'd brought for Christmas Eve. "I cannot imagine how *cats* got in there."

"As she said, it's a mystery," Colin said lightly.

Too lightly, Amy thought. Turning to drape the dress over a chair, she slanted him a glance and caught the satisfied look on his face.

"You did it, didn't you?" she accused with a gasp. "Somehow, while we were skating, you let cats into your sister's room."

"I did not," he protested, looking entirely too innocent.

Only someone guilty could contrive to look *that* blameless.

Knowing him, she waited.

She didn't have to wait long. "But Margaret might have," he added with a hint of a devilish grin.

"Margaret?"

"Kendra's maid, the short girl with the big blue eyes? I had to bribe her to get her to cooperate, but she seems to be enjoying our caper immensely."

Amy's first instinct was to righteously admonish him, but of course that was due to the tension between them. She'd known he was a shameless prankster when she married him. It was one of the many things she loved about him—no matter that she often claimed otherwise—and if their differences had been settled, she'd be laughing.

Instead, she tried and failed to hide a smile. "Pray tell, what is the aim of this caper?"

"To keep Kendra and Trick apart. We've strewn their room with pungent cheese, given them drinks to make them sleep, taken their door off its hinges—" When she gasped again, he grinned outright and shook his head. "Kendra brought this on herself. She should have known better than to discuss her love life in my hearing."

"She didn't know you were there," Amy protested mildly. "And this last prank was mean. You've seen how much cats make her sneeze."

He shrugged. "Harmless fun, and I've been sorely in need of fun." Her guilt sparked, she opened her mouth to retort, but he held up a hand. "Perhaps it has gone far enough. I'm done. I'll leave them alone tonight. Just tell me you're willing to keep this quiet until I'm ready to reveal the truth."

"Of course I am," she said, reaching behind her back to tug at her laces. "I wouldn't dream of destroying your amusement. I only wonder why she and Trick haven't figured out what's been going on."

"I expect they're consumed with other thoughts," he said, one eyebrow raised suggestively. "Can I help you with that?" Without waiting for an answer, he stepped behind her and changed the subject. "Next Christmas, we'll be able to bring all of our attendants to Jason's place."

"Where they'll get lost in Cainewood's ninety-eight rooms once again," she predicted with a little laugh. "But I don't mind not having Agnes here. She was so happy to spend Christmas with her family." Feeling his deft fingers loosen her laces reminded her of their first weeks together, when they'd started their married life with only Benchley on their staff. "And I suppose it's not so bad having you take her place for a while."

"I'm enjoying taking her place." He swept her hair aside and kissed her neck, partially dissolving the frisson of vexation she often felt with him these days. "It was a lovely day," he murmured against her skin. "Thank you for not arguing with Aidan."

"I gave you my word," she said. "There's no need to thank me for keeping a promise."

His fingers fumbled, which she hoped meant he felt remorse for not keeping his own word. But the truth was that she wouldn't have argued with Aidan today whether she'd promised or not.

Because she was no longer sure what to say to him.

As Colin eased her bodice off her shoulders, she heard Kendra's voice in her head for what seemed like the hundredth time...

I remember you telling me how unfair it was, that your father was dictating your life instead of letting you live it—and—what your father did to you, well...you're doing the same thing to your own child...

Was she?

Those words had hit her in the gut.

She didn't know how she would have responded had the children not burst in with news that the pond had frozen, drawing everyone's attention. But she'd been able to think of little since.

"Hey," Colin said softly, interrupting her ruminations. His warm hands on her bared shoulders, he turned her to face him. "I gave you my word, too. And I...I've decided to keep my promise," he rushed out, searching her eyes for approval. "I only ask that we wait till we're home to tell Aidan."

It was the last thing she'd expected to hear from him. "Really?" she breathed, searching his eyes in return.

"Really."

Her heart melted right then and there, and her arms went around him. Never mind that she was no longer sure she wanted to go through with her original plans, his willingness to support her meant everything.

"Aidan may be unhappy for a while," Colin continued, "but you're right, he'll survive. And it's not as though he has any better prospects. I have no idea what I'd be doing these days if Charles hadn't given me the earldom." Charles II, he meant. Upon his restoration in 1660, the king had awarded land and titles to all three Chase brothers, as thanks for their family's support. "A rather unprecedented piece of luck—we second sons rarely find our places so easily."

In truth, life hadn't proved easy for Colin at all—not during his childhood, and not later, either. In part thanks to wedding her, he'd struggled mightily to make his estate profitable and restore the small, crumbling castle where they now lived so cozily. But she'd learned early on that he was determined to turn every disadvantage life dealt him into a benefit. He believed hard work and dedication were the best means to a happy ending. That attitude was admirable, and another of his many qualities that had made her fall in love with him.

"I'm sure Aidan would find something to do with his life," she pointed out, playing devil's advocate while she hugged him tight. "Countless second sons seem to get by one way or another."

He shrugged and squeezed her back. "Perhaps. But my honor will not survive disappointing you. My word means everything, as you've been trying to tell me for months. I cannot betray you. I regret my failure to see that earlier."

"A Chase promise is not given lightly," she murmured, hearing Jason say so in her memory. A statement he'd made when she'd first arrived at Cainewood, newly orphaned by the Great Fire of London, more than twenty-two years ago.

"No, it's never given lightly," Colin agreed. "Most especially to those we love."

It wasn't the first time she'd heard those words from him, and perhaps that was why they echoed in her heart now.

Reconciled at last, the two of them just gazed at each other for a long, melting moment. A measure of peace settled over them, a comforting serenity they'd been missing the past months. His lips found their way to hers, and hers to his, instinctively after so much time together. As they kissed, his hands skimmed down her arms, pushing her gown to puddle on the floor.

At first she assumed he was just helping her undress to change. But then he began backing her toward the bed.

A sharp knock came at the door.

"Yes?" Colin all but barked.

It opened a crack. "My lord," Benchley called, "I wish not to intrude—"

"Then don't."

"I've been told I must move your things."

"You'll have all night. Go away. For at least an hour," Colin added loudly as the door shut.

His mouth went to hers again.

"The caroling," she protested weakly.

"A pox on the caroling…"

TWENTY-SIX

JEWEL

EARING HER most Christmasy gown, made of red taffeta over a white under-skirt embroidered with gold, Jewel returned to the main house to find the drawing room in something of a tumult.

"Uncle Jason isn't in the stables," young Rebecca was reporting in a panic. "And neither are the cats!"

Finding it difficult to contain her amusement, Jewel watched Aunty Kendra and Uncle Trick troop in, much earlier than everyone expected. Her aunt's new gown was indeed elaborate—a confection of gold satin with silver lace spilling from the sleeves—but apparently it hadn't taken her as long to don as she'd anticipated, Jewel thought.

Well, actually, that's what she hoped *everyone else* thought.

Because she knew the truth was—

"There are cats in my chamber!" Kendra announced before the door even closed behind her. "Cats!"

"Egad!" Aunty Violet cried, apparently sharing Rebecca's panic for a moment before visibly pulling herself together and taking charge.

She whirled to her daughter. "Rebecca, go round up those creatures once again. Take some cousins with you."

She looked to Kendra. "I'm so sorry! I'll have Harry and Hilda dispatch every non-kitchen servant to scour your chamber from top to bottom."

"We're swapping rooms with Colin and Amy," Kendra informed her.

But Violet was already marching from the room, calling, "Start the caroling!" behind her.

Rebecca collected six cousins, who all bundled up and left, followed by a steady stream of servants with mops and brooms in hand.

Not usually one to follow orders, Aunty Kendra nevertheless plopped onto the harpsichord's bench and placed her hands on the keyboard. Jewel had never seen her look so…

Frustrated? Stunned? Confused?

Jewel couldn't be sure, but one thing was certain: This was a masterful prank.

She struggled to hide a smile as, by fits and starts, the rest of the family drifted in, gathered around, and began singing carols.

Well, except for her parents…

TWENTY-SEVEN

AMY

"*A* POX ON *the caroling*" was enough to persuade Amy.

She wanted to give in.

It seemed a long time since she and Colin had made love without the strain of conflict between them. Much, much too long a time.

She'd already removed her shoes and stockings, and her gown was a puddle on the floor. With impatient hands, he pulled her chemise off over her head, nearly ripping it in the process. After making short work of divesting his own clothing, he eased her down to the bed, running his fingers through her dark tresses and arranging them artistically on the pillows before coming down beside her.

He gathered her into his arms and for a moment just held her close.

In the still room, she could feel his heart beating against hers.

When he brushed the hair off her forehead and framed her face with his hands, his emerald eyes shone with such a deep, abiding love that her breath caught in her chest. With a soft groan, he covered her parted lips with his own. His tongue plundered her mouth with reckless abandon, until both of them were breathless.

Her heart swelling with emotion, she raised a hand to skim his muscled chest, his sleek side, the smooth planes of his broad back. Everything about him felt divine, yet also comforting and familiar. Her fingers traced the scar on his arm, a reminder that he'd become a skilled swordsman many years before they met. Enjoying the warm expanse of his skin, she brushed her palm down his side to his hip, then edged around to find him hard and ready.

"No," Colin whispered, his mouth against hers. "Not today." He reached down to remove her hand, to lace his fingers with hers, to bring their joined hands to his lips. "This is for you, my love. Consider it my apology."

Owing to all of his years with her, all of their minutes and hours and days spent together in love, there were few things he knew better than how to make her respond to him. What could she do but give in and let him take over? Let him take her where he would?

For long, sweet minutes he played her body, making her senses careen with the consummate deftness of a master. Every intimate stroke of his fingers, every burning trail of his lips sent currents of desire pulsing through her, awakening the memories of him that she always carried with her, deep in her heart, all of the shared experiences that defined them through the ups and downs of their life together.

At long last he moved over her and glided down, the roughness on his chin and cheek grazing against her softness, his mouth hot and wet on her skin. His lips traversed her sensitive inner thighs, leaving a damp, fiery trail of kisses in their wake. Tantalizingly warm, his breath washed over her before the tip of his tongue touched her, tearing a ragged sob from her throat.

She trembled uncontrollably, lifting her hips to get closer still. As his mouth teased her mercilessly, she felt the blood coursing through her veins, spreading the familiar tingling weakness everywhere. She twisted beneath him, crying out his name.

He lifted his head. She opened her eyes and gazed down at him.

The eyes that blazed into hers were a deep, fathomless green, overflowing with emotion that words could never convey. His breath came in a deep, ragged rhythm as he hovered there, and she could feel his life force sluicing through his veins, to match the insistent throbbing between her legs.

"Now," she said, her voice shaky and tremulous. "This is for you, too. For both of us. Come inside me now. Please."

He hesitated, clearly torn between his intentions and her desires. "If you wish," he whispered at last.

"I *demand*."

"Well, then…" He came over her and slid inside her welcoming body with a single swift thrust.

Amy let out a long, soft moan. Having him there felt so right that tears of gratitude came to her eyes. He kissed her, his mouth urgent and hungry, and she tasted herself on his lips. He rocked against her, his hips maneuvering in a rhythm as ancient as time, and she matched his every move. She could feel him holding back, feel the uneven tempo of his breath as he struggled for control, feel the staccato beat of his heart against hers.

And then, with a groan of capitulation, he let go, and she felt him pulsing inside her. Feeling her own contractions burst forth, matching and melding with his, she arched herself closer, wanting him deeper, the two of them so in rhythm that she couldn't tell where one of them stopped and the other started.

A while later, once their hearts had slowed, he came up on his elbows and brushed the tangled curls off her face with reverent hands. His lips grazed her eyelids, her forehead, one ear. "I love you," he whispered there.

"I love you, too," she whispered fiercely. Her arms

tightened around him, crushing him to her. She kissed him with all the exquisite tenderness she felt in her heart, completely at peace for the first time in months.

"Tell me again," she begged, putting a smile in her voice.

"I love you," he said simply, and she didn't doubt it.

Not for a moment.

TWENTY-EIGHT

JEWEL

BY THE TIME Jewel's parents returned and took their places near the harpsichord, Uncle Ford's tall case clock had chimed the quarter-hours at least three times, maybe four. Which meant that more than an hour had passed.

An hour filled with lackluster caroling.

Jewel observed a marked lack of enthusiasm, especially compared to the family's singing yesterday. She wished they could stop, and even ventured to suggest it, but Aunty Violet was insistent.

The light had faded, and candles had been lit. Despite Violet's valiant efforts to keep mulled wine flowing and holiday nibbles nearby, Jewel heard stomachs rumbling. It was well past time for supper.

Unfortunately, Uncle Jason still hadn't appeared. No doubt feeling pressured by expectations, Aunty Cait had changed into a fancy turquoise gown that looked too bright for her current demeanor. She was curled miserably in an oversized chair.

As often happened during family gatherings, Jewel was wedged on a couch between eighteen-year-old Elspeth and sixteen-year-old Diana. Outnumbered by uncouth boys, the older girls had always stuck together. Diana plaited Jewel's hair over and over while the desultory caroling droned on.

When a loud banging of the door knocker interrupted, Jewel found herself immensely relieved.

"Jason!" Aunty Cait cried, jumping up from her curled misery.

"I'll get him," Uncle Ford said and left the room.

But it wasn't Uncle Jason at the door. Instead, Ford returned with...

Jewel blinked.

Rowan Ashcroft?

Could that tall man be her childhood friend Rowan, Aunty Violet's brother?

Although her family visited Uncle Ford and Aunty Violet rather regularly, Jewel hadn't seen Rowan in what felt like forever. Certainly more than a decade, and that had suited her just fine. Quite recently, in a casual conversation, Henry had mentioned that he and Rowan were friends—which she'd found a little unsettling, because she'd done her best to put Rowan out of her mind.

Diana's fingers ceased plaiting. A hubbub broke out as everyone rose. Ford's children squealed, running to hug their youngest uncle.

"What a welcome!" Rowan told them, gathering the three youngsters into his arms. "I'm so happy to see you all, too."

"Who is *that?*" Elspeth whispered to Jewel.

"Their uncle." Jewel pulled her fingers through her hair to unravel it. "Aunty Violet's little brother."

"Little?" Diana scoffed. "He's so tall! And so handsome!"

"You can have him," Jewel muttered as Rowan finally disentangled himself and glanced around.

Unfortunately, she couldn't drop into the floor or otherwise disappear. Also unfortunately, he noticed her nearly immediately.

"Good evening, Jewel," he said. He looked to her left. "And Lord and Lady Greystone," he added, walking toward her parents. "You two never seem to age."

As he reached them, he bowed and kissed her mother's hand, smooth as silk.

Beside Jewel, Elspeth all but swooned.

"Lord Tremayne." Mama all but glowed. "It's a pleasure to see you after all these years."

"The pleasure is mine," Rowan returned, a twinkle in his emerald green eyes.

He'd changed. He'd grown up. His voice was deeper than Jewel remembered, his shoulders wider. Unlike her family, he wasn't dressed up for the holiday festivities, but his blue-black hair skimmed the collar of a perfectly cut midnight blue suit that was appropriate for traveling.

Her mother was still beaming at him, clearly captivated.

Well, he could captivate Mama and Elspeth and Diana, but he wasn't going to captivate Jewel. He hadn't captivated her since she was ten.

"What are you doing here?" she asked bluntly.

"Yes, what are you doing here?" Aunty Violet echoed with a puzzled frown.

"Ford invited me for Christmas Eve supper."

"He did?" She turned to her husband. "You did?"

Uncle Ford looked wary. "Your mother thought you'd enjoy the surprise."

"Ha!" she said with a huff. "I suspect she feared I'd see through her matchmaking machinations." Wondering what she had meant by *matchmaking machinations*, Jewel watched Aunty Violet put a smile on her face. "It's not that I don't want you here, Rowan. But I'd have appreciated some notice. And you'd have been late if we'd started on time."

"I'm sorry," Ford and Rowan said simultaneously.

Despite herself, Aunty Violet laughed. "Well, there's no sense in sitting here hungry all night. I'll go tell Hilda to set another place, then we'll begin whether Jason has returned or not."

As Violet departed, Rowan moved closer. "How are you, Jewel?" he asked, reaching for her hand.

In unison, her cousins dropped back onto the couch, gazing up at him with dreamy expressions. When Jewel tried to draw her hand away, he held on tighter and raised it, bending to press his lips to the back. Warm lips. She heard the girls' sharply indrawn breaths, and her skin seemed to tighten, like it had when she was a child.

Like it hadn't since. How annoying.

She was really better off avoiding him.

"I see you're still working with glass," he said, looking down at her hand with all of its little wounds in various stages of healing.

"Yes." She tugged it free, clasping it together with her other. "But the cuts don't hurt."

"You always said that."

"I don't want to talk to you, Rowan," she said, surprised at her own rudeness.

"And why is that?" he wondered, having the gall to look hurt while her cousins drank in his every word. "We were so close when we were young. Why all of a sudden did you decide I am worse than a case of head lice? I'm aware that at a certain age girls are obligated to hate boys, but certainly you've long since outgrown that folly."

How could he not know? "Do you not remember saying something that might have convinced me to keep my distance?"

"No." He frowned, his gaze narrowing. "No. If I hurt your feelings, I apologize. But whatever could I have said?"

He didn't remember? Her memory of that day was still powerful enough to instantly bring heat to her cheeks, but he didn't even remember.

Splendid. Just *perfect*.

She could recall Rowan's exact words, for they had been burned into her childish, love-addled brain. More than a decade ago, after his sister's wedding, the women in Rowan's family had been bantering about the future, blithely planning his wedding to—

"Jewel?" Young Rowan's emerald eyes had widened in alarm. "I'm not going to marry Jewel!"

He'd gazed upon Jewel with such horror, she'd shrunk back.

She'd wanted to die.

She'd wished the earth would open up and swallow her.

Rowan's newly married brother-in-law had aimed an indulgent smile down at him. "You're only eleven. Wait till you're older—"

"Never! I'm not going to marry Jewel! NEVER!"

Those words had haunted her for months. Years,

even, for she'd spent much of her adolescence convinced she was unlovable. It had seemed that if the boy she loved—or thought she loved—could reject her in such a public and hurtful way, there had to be something wrong with her.

Whilst she had long since realized she was worthy of love, long since let go of the pain he had caused, she had never forgotten those words.

But apparently Rowan had.

The worst day of her childhood had meant less than nothing to him.

A bell rang, saving her from answering. "The holiday supper is about to begin," she said stiffly, suspecting her face was as red as her gown. "I must take my seat."

In a swish of crackling taffeta, she turned and made her way to the dining room, sensing him following behind her.

TWENTY-NINE

CAITHREN

*C*AITHREN WASN'T hungry.

Not even for plum pudding (not that any had been served yet).

Jason still hadn't shown up. Although she had a little of everything on the plate that sat before her, she felt too anxious to eat. She was sure she couldn't swallow past the lump in her throat. If Jason didn't return soon, she didn't know what she would do with herself.

Still and all, she couldn't help noticing that Christmas Eve Supper was a veritable feast.

One of the advantages of taking turns hosting Christmas was the menu changed from year to year. Tonight's table was laden with all of Violet's family's favorite holiday dishes: A colossal Christmas pie filled with turkey, chicken, and bacon swimming in butter; fish cooked in wine and butter; buttered cauliflower seasoned with cinnamon; buttered artichoke hearts seasoned with ginger; and a potato pudding swirled with butter, onions, and spices. Beside an enormous bowl of sallet, hot loaves of fresh white manchet bread sat on a board with a knife.

And a large crock of butter, of course.

Despite her misery, the second thing she couldn't help noticing was the overabundance of butter.

And there was a third thing she couldn't help noticing: Rowan enchanting half the ladies at the table.

His mastery was a sight to behold.

"When did your brother become so sleekit?" she asked Violet in a whisper.

"So sleekit?"

"So charming. Such a heartbreaker."

"Oh." Violet chuckled in Cait's ear. "Sometime between Eton and Oxford. He flirts with everything in a skirt."

Elspeth and Diana were hanging on his every word. Even Amy looked a wee bit enthralled. "Only Jewel seems immune," Cait observed.

"Beg pardon, my lady." A footman appeared beside her. "The marquess waits in the drawing room and requests your presence."

"Oh!" Her heart suddenly racing, she jumped up and rushed through the lobby and into the adjacent room.

When she found Jason standing there, looking pale, she flung herself at him, then swiftly pulled back. "Crivvens, you're cold. So cold."

He just shrugged.

"Oh, Jason, I'm so sorry..." She wanted to say she was sorry she'd kept the secret, but she couldn't bring herself to do it when she didn't know what he was thinking. Instead, fraught with nerves, she took an embroidered blanket off the couch and wrapped it around his shoulders. "How did you get so cold?"

"I walked for hours," he said as she drew him over to the fire. "Just thinking. I can only remember doing that one other time. Before we were wed. The time I thought I'd lost you."

"By all the saints," she whispered. "Can you ever forgive me?" Her heart was pounding. "I know I've made a terrible mess of things. But it's Christmas, and I didn't want to upset you, and I couldn't bear to think —" Hearing herself blethering, she broke off and drew a deep breath. "I'm so sorry, Jase. I didn't mean to get with child—"

"Oh, really? *That's* what you're sorry for?" He stared down at her in disbelief. "Do you suppose you got with child on your own?"

"Nay, I—I did not mean that I'm at fault. Just that I'm sorry it's happened and—"

"What?" He looked, if possible, even more incredulous. "Cait, what are you saying? Do you not *want* this child?"

"Of course I do!" Tears pricked her eyes at the thought of how much she loved and wanted the bairn growing inside her. "You were so excited," she choked out, fighting to keep her composure, "looking forward to our—our next chapter. Traveling without little ones. Just the two of us. You couldn't wait, and I couldn't bear to bring you the news that would ruin your happiness—and at Christmas, no less. You said"—he pressed a handkerchief into her hand, and she blew her nose noisily—"you said that getting me with child would be a *calamity!*"

"Oh, Cait. You took that seriously?" He let her blow her nose once more, then gripped her shoulders and made her look at him. "Sweet Cait, I want our child as much as you do." As more tears leaked down her face, his jaw clenched. "But you should have told me. I'm hurt that you didn't tell me. I'm hurt you told others before me. You did that once before, when you were carrying Griffin, when you feared I'd cancel our journey to Scotland. And you promised you'd never keep a pregnancy from me again."

"I tried to tell you, more than once, but I just

couldn't do it. I couldn't make myself do it. I was so afraid..."

"Of what?" he asked, his gaze filled with confusion.

For a moment, they both fell silent. Muffled laughter came from the dining room, so at odds with the tension between them.

"Oh, Cait." As Jason stepped closer, the embroidered blanket slid from his shoulders to the floor. "You've done to me what I once did to you. And you were hurt then, or so you said."

As always, he was calm in his anger. In all of their years together, he'd never raised his voice to her. Blinking back more tears, she hugged herself. "I'm not sure what you're talking about." She couldn't think straight.

"I didn't trust you to understand that I'd killed your brother accidentally. I didn't trust you not to hold that accidental death against me. Can you not see, Cait? You're doing the same thing here. Not trusting me to accept this accidental pregnancy with understanding... and joy."

"Joy?" She couldn't have heard him right. Her eyes widened through the tears. "*Joy?*"

"Yes, joy," he repeated firmly. "All three of our children bring me joy. Why should this one be any different?"

He sounded sincere. But she was afraid to believe

him. "I feared this one might be different because, well... because..."

She had to know.

"Would you feel the same way if I hadn't already conceived?" she rushed out. "Would you still want another child? Its arrival will delay the future you've been envisioning—mightn't some part of you resent that? And perhaps resent the child because of it?"

He shook his head, looking thoroughly disgusted. "See, there you go questioning my motives again. I'm devastated you don't think better of me. I would gladly have ten more children with you, delaying that future for decades. I only talked of that because it seemed our family was complete—"

"Silent dugs also bite," she cut in quietly.

"Pardon? Is that yet another of your mother's endless cryptic sayings?"

"Aye. Her way of saying we should assume nothing in this life."

"Well, I did assume, but I'm happy to learn I was wrong. Another child is a blessing."

"I assumed, too—that I knew how you'd react. And I'm thrilled to be wrong."

Quite suddenly, she realized just how very wrong she'd been. After twenty-one years with this man, how had she thought he might not love another child? She'd seen nothing in him to suggest that could happen. *Nothing.* What on earth had she been thinking?

"Oh, Jase," she said. "I cannot believe the things I just said to you. I didn't mean any of it. I think pregnancy must be making me daft."

"It wouldn't be the first time," he said with a hint of his usual good humor. "Thank God it's temporary. Will it help if I tell you I love you both sane and daft?"

A trickle of relief coursed through her blood. A tremulous hope began to rise. "Does that mean you'll forgive me?"

"I will." He fixed her with a fierce green gaze. "So long as you promise never to underestimate me again."

She remembered telling him something similar, long ago, before she allowed him to propose. "I promise," she told him solemnly, then launched herself into his arms.

His embrace was the most welcome thing she'd felt in recent memory. He held her so tight she could feel the pendant he wore on a chain beneath his shirt—the emerald amulet that had come down through her family. "Another babe, sweet," he murmured, sounding genuinely pleased. "The Gypsy was right."

"Hmm?" More laughter from the dining room filled her heart with happiness now. Loving the family she'd joined with this man, she snuggled even closer. "What Gypsy?"

"The one who sold me your wedding ring."

"Oh, aye." She pulled her left arm from around him to see it on her hand—a flat engraved band embedded with tiny, bright green emeralds. "You bought it without dickering," she reminded him with a wee smile.

"She also told your fortune. She said you'd have a happy marriage. And *four* children."

When Cait looked up, her astonished laugh that bubbled up was covered by his kiss.

THIRTY

JEWEL

J EWEL LICKED her lips, perusing the selection of sweets.

More than a few now graced the Christmas Eve table, including creamy custard, spiced gingerbread, sugared almonds, and a platter of marzipan shaped into tiny edible sculptures of berries, fruits, and wreaths. There was also a giant strawberry tart, courtesy of Aunty Violet's father's greenhouse.

Aunty Kendra already had some of everything on her plate. Across the table, Diana and Elspeth were busily choosing sweetmeats for Rowan, having contrived to sit on either side of him. But the plum pudding had yet to appear, because two family members were missing.

186 | LAUREN ROYAL

"We've all been waiting for you for the pudding!" Jewel's cousin Adam told his parents when they finally entered the dining room.

"Your father hasn't eaten." Aunty Cait was fairly glowing with renewed good humor. "You'll have to wait a wee bit longer."

"No one has to wait," Uncle Jason disagreed as he took his seat. "I'll eat the rest of this fish and some Christmas pie while everyone else enjoys the plum pudding. I don't want to keep *anyone* from their pudding—most especially my dear, pregnant wife, who's been craving plum pudding for days."

Jewel wasn't the only one who gasped at that news, although she noticed that none of the older generation seemed surprised. "Then let's not keep Cait waiting!" Aunty Violet exclaimed as she rose from her chair. "I'll go tell Hilda we're ready for the pudding."

After Violet left, the chamber was conspicuously quiet for a moment.

A very short moment.

"You're having a *baby*?" Aunty Cait's eldest son burst out. "After all this time?" He exchanged glances with his brothers. All three of them seemed in shock. "How did that happen?"

"Honestly, Griffin?" the youngest, Jamie, scoffed. He was fourteen. "Even *I* know how *that* happened."

General laughter broke out, followed by a hubbub of questions and congratulations. But all of that abruptly

ceased when the plum pudding was brought in flaming
and they began singing "Sir Christèmas," a tradition
that Violet had brought to the family long ago.

"Nowell, nowell, nowell, nowell
Who is there that singeth so: Nowell, nowell?
I am here, Sir Christèmas.
Welcome, my lord Sir Christèmas!
Welcome to all, both more and less!
Come near, come near.
Nowell, nowell."

To Jewel, the room felt magical with all of their
voices raised in melodious song. The fathomless darkness beyond the windows seemed to magnify the soft,
warm candlelight inside and the brighter flames that
danced around the lit pudding.

"Dieu vous garde, beaux sieurs, tidings I you bring:
A maid hath borne a child full young,
Which causeth you to sing: Nowell, nowell.
Christ is now born of a pure maid;
In an ox-stall he is laid,
Wherefore sing we at abrayde: Nowell, nowell.
Buvez bien, buvez bien par toute la compagnie.
Make good cheer and be right merry,
And sing with us now joyfully: Nowell, nowell.
Nowell."

188 | LAUREN ROYAL

As the verse came to an end, a hush fell over the chamber. Jewel savored the comfortable silence for the brief time it lasted, until a footman stepped forward to take the pudding to be sliced and served.

"Now it feels like Christmas is really here," she declared.

"It truly does," Rowan agreed, the sparkle in his deep green eyes annoying her for some reason she couldn't fathom. "Did you know that Christmas pudding was banned by Oliver Cromwell? He believed the ritual of flaming harked back to pagan celebrations of the winter solstice. My parents met during that time, when celebrating Christmas wasn't allowed. Not that that stopped my mother," he added with a flirtatious wink.

She tried to glance away, but he was still looking at her, clearly expecting her to say something. Vexed, she shifted on her seat. "Thank you for the history lesson," she muttered ungraciously.

A puzzled frown crossed Elspeth's features before she turned to him and touched his arm. "What did your mother do?" she asked brightly, drawing his attention.

Which was fine with Jewel. She wanted nothing to do with Rowan.

Why was that?

Once upon a time, she'd have been thrilled to have him flirt with her. While he regaled his adoring audience with his mother's antics during the time Christmas was outlawed, she tried to figure out why he aggravated her now.

Many years ago he'd hurt her, but at twenty-one, she was old enough to know he hadn't hurt her on purpose. What had felt like cruel rejection at ten had been no more than a boy being a boy, and a rather typical boy, at that—she'd watched her own brothers behave the same way at that age, after all. That Rowan hadn't remembered the incident shouldn't have come as a surprise, given how little it had meant to him. And although she'd been terribly rude to him from the moment he'd walked in the door, he was being perfectly nice to her.

In fact, he was perfectly nice to everyone. Even Elspeth and Diana, who were both acting like lovesick ninnies.

Since when had he become so nice? In truth, Jewel decided, "perfectly nice" didn't even *begin* to describe grown-up Rowan.

He was *too* nice.

Maybe *that* was what irked her.

Henry was nice, but not so nice he charmed everyone in his sphere. Rowan's abundance of niceness couldn't be real. It had to be disingenuous. A performance.

She'd all but told him he had hurt her. Only a dunce wouldn't hear the message implied in *"Do you not remember saying something that might have convinced me to keep my distance?"* And Rowan was no dunce. That much she remembered.

Was he performing for her benefit? Trying to prove he wouldn't hurt her again? Trying to make up for hurting her in the past?

If so, she thought as a slice of the plum pudding was set before her, she was a deplorable human being. Because she didn't want to make up with him.

She wanted to hurt him back.

"Mmmm,"Aunty Cait murmured appreciatively, having already dug into her own pudding, which was drenched in glimmering hard sauce. "Mmm, mmmm. Crivvens, I do believe this tastes better than ever before."

A little smile curved Mama's lips. "Thank you," she said modestly. "Since I'm hopeless in the kitchen and have been tweaking this recipe for years, my Aunt Elizabeth offered to help me figure the measurements. She sent her suggestions all the way from Paris. I think I've finally got it right."

"Was it your mother's recipe?" Rowan asked her.

"Oh, my, no." Mama laughed. "My family always kept a cook—I doubt my mother knew how to boil water. I found the plum pudding recipe at Greystone, tucked into an old book in the library. That happened nearly twenty years ago, and I've been tweaking it ever since"—she laughed again—"which just goes to prove I inherited my mother's lack of culinary talent."

"Well, it's perfect now," Aunty Cait said. "Have you written down what you did this year?"

"Oh, yes," Jewel confirmed. "She took copious notes."

"Then we won't want to lose those notes." Looking thoughtful, Caithren took a small sip of mulled wine. "I think we should start a Chase receipt book. We'll begin with the plum pudding. Every Christmas we can each bring a new recipe to add to the book."

"Or an old one," Aunty Kendra agreed enthusiastically. "But all sweets. I think all the recipes should be for sweets."

"Of course you do," Uncle Ford put in with a roll of his eyes. "Your preference for sweets is legendary."

Before Aunty Kendra could retort, Jewel's cousin Jamie yelled, "Found something!" He fished a flat, round piece from his mouth. "A silver penny!"

"That means you have a fortune in the offing," Mama told him with a smile.

His eldest brother fixed him with a superior glare. "You'll *need* a fortune," he stated gleefully, "since you're a third son."

Apparently Griffin had been peeved by Jamie insinuating he didn't know where babies came from.

Raising her cup, Aunty Kendra deftly changed the subject. "I think this delicious mulled wine would be a good addition to our family receipt book."

"There's a story about that mulled wine," Aunty

Violet said. "My mother made a batch with my father before he proposed. He changed the recipe, and now she swears it inspires love." Holding her own cup aloft, she looked to her brother Rowan. And then to Jewel.

Everyone laughed.

Except Jewel.

She sipped from her cup of mulled wine, hiding a frown. How irritating it was that everyone seemed to think she should be romantically interested in Rowan. Henry was much nicer than Rowan.

Unlike Rowan, Henry was *genuinely* nice.

Henry hadn't broken her heart.

Henry had never hurt her.

"Maybe we should include little stories in our family receipt book," Aunty Cait suggested. "This one about the mulled wine, and Amy, do you have a story about the plum pudding?"

"Only that it took me nearly twenty years to get the recipe right."

"There's more, Mama," Hugh interjected. "Remember how you always say the Stir-Up Sunday wishes come true?"

"That's lovely," Aunty Cait said. "A bonnie tradition."

"Then it's settled," Aunty Kendra decided. "Every year at Christmas, each lady will bring a recipe with a story or legend behind it. For a sweet."

Aunty Cait squealed. "The wishbone!" she cried around a mouthful of pudding. "Again!"

"Again?" Uncle Jason's brows knitted in confusion. "When's the last time you found a wishbone in plum pudding, given that you haven't eaten any in more than a decade?"

"Um…"

Aunty Kendra cleared her throat. "She might have sneaked some pudding yesterday. Maybe."

"What?" Aunty Cait's three boys chimed in unison.

"Oh, heavens," Aunty Kendra said. "What does it matter? Clearly she was meant to find the wishbone regardless," she added before anyone could tell her why it mattered. "It's a sign of luck! It means she'll have her girl at last." She turned to her eldest brother. "Jason, are you looking forward to having a daughter?"

"I'll believe we'll have a daughter when I'm holding her," he said.

Aunty Cait nodded emphatically.

And everyone laughed again.

The genial family harmony flowed into Jewel like warm honey. She loved her family, loved the thought of creating her own new family to blend with all of her loved ones here.

For the first time in days, she was feeling happy. Relaxed. Content.

Young Rebecca found something next. "A thimble!" she exclaimed.

"A life of blessedness," Jewel's mother told her.

"Truly?" Rebecca's twin, Marcus, raised a brow. "Then this whole thing is stupid, because everyone knows Rebecca is the *least* saintly person in this room."

"Egad, Marc!" Aunty Violet chided. "What a thing to say about your sister. And at Christmas, no less."

Well, maybe the family wasn't precisely harmonious. But the bickering wasn't ruining Jewel's happiness. She loved the bickering, too.

"Look, I got the anchor," Aidan announced. "Which is patently ridiculous," he added beneath his breath.

"Because you made it?" Jewel whispered beside him.

"Because it symbolizes safe harbor, and the *last* thing I feel right now is safe."

He'd said that a little too loudly. Jewel's gaze shot to her mother. She looked upset. Or maybe she looked chagrined. Or she might be feeling a few other things, but it was quite clear that none of them were positive.

Jewel spooned more pudding into her mouth, feeling sympathy for Mama, but also annoyance that she was pushing Aidan into a life he didn't want.

The annoyance might be stronger. She couldn't quite decide; perhaps the mulled wine was making it hard to tell. But although she'd stayed out of her parents' disagreement so far, as Aidan's big sister she felt she should say something.

Then, before she could open her mouth to say she-didn't-know-what, she bit into something hard and knew what it was immediately. "Oh, no," she said instead, holding up the pudding-encrusted ring. "Someone else was meant to get this, given that I have no plans to marry anytime soon."

Mama sighed, looking even more despondent.

Jewel hated seeing her so unhappy.

"No plans to marry? What a shame," Rowan said in his obnoxious flirtatious tone.

Jewel's teeth ground together. She wanted to wipe the smile off his face.

Looking between her mother's crestfallen face and Rowan's genial one, something came over her. Something rather mad—or perhaps mulled. "I was only jesting," she found herself saying. "I *was* meant to get this ring. The Viscount Copthorne has asked me to marry him, and I've decided to accept."

Excited gasps filled the air.

"He proposed before asking your father?" Mama burst out. But in opposition to her mood a moment ago, she looked thrilled.

"Well, he didn't propose, exactly. He asked if I would object to him asking Papa." Feeling lighter than she had in days, Jewel looked to her father. "Please don't tell him I told you that. Allow him to ask you properly, I beg you."

"There's no need to beg, poppet. I'm happy to keep your secret. My little girl is to be wed!"

And with that, both of her parents jumped up and

rounded the table to embrace her, and a hubbub of chatter and congratulations broke out once more.

A baby and a betrothal—what a momentous night this was turning out to be!

"Henry Breckenridge?"

One voice stood out among the commotion. Rowan's. Jewel disentangled herself from her parents to find him staring at her.

Far from looking flirtatious, he crossed his arms. "You're marrying *Henry Breckenridge?*"

The chamber went silent.

"Aren't the two of you friends?" Baffled, Jewel blinked. "Didn't you attend Oxford together? I'm nearly certain he told me that."

"Yes, Oxford. And Eton. Yes, we are friends. Good friends."

She shot a puzzled glance to her parents before looking back to him. "Why shouldn't I marry Henry? What's wrong with him?"

"Nothing. He's just…not right for you."

"How would you know what's right for me, Rowan? I'm not the same girl I was at age ten."

And Rowan sure wasn't the same boy.

"I don't know how I would know," he mumbled, strikingly out of character with the smooth Rowan she'd seen earlier. "I just think…he's just…" He cleared his throat. "He's Catholic."

"He comes from a Catholic family, yes." She looked

again to her parents and felt relieved when they both nodded, indicating they didn't find that a concern. "But he's willing to wed in the Church of England."

Rowan glanced around, as though he were searching the walls for another objection. "The Breckenridges don't support William and Mary taking the throne."

"Unfortunately for them, King James isn't fighting to keep it." Pleased to see how off-balanced she'd made him, she smiled and cocked her head. "Anything else?"

"Yes. No. I mean, never mind." He shifted uncomfortably. "Marry whomever you want."

Jewel couldn't help rolling her eyes. "I wasn't aware I needed your permission."

"Now that *that's* settled," Aunty Violet put in quickly, "and the last token has been found, shall we all fetch our gifts?"

"And that's my cue to leave," Rowan told her, rising from the table.

She turned to him, looking perplexed. "Why on earth would you leave?"

"I don't have gifts for anyone. And I suspect I'm not wanted here," he added, his gaze darting to Jewel and back.

She felt a flash of triumph. It wasn't complete revenge—he wasn't in love with her, after all, so she couldn't very well hurt him as badly as he'd hurt her.

But it was something.

Aunty Violet was not giving up. "Rowan, that's not—"

"There's no room here for me to sleep," he insisted. "Every chamber is overflowing. I'm going to Father and Mum's house. I'll see you there tomorrow."

"Rowan—"

"Let him go, Violet," Uncle Ford said. "Good Lord, they're just next door." A slight exaggeration—though the Trentingham estate shared a border with Lakefield, that border was a mile away. "Fetch your things, Rowan, and then we'll see you off and join you at noon. Everyone else, bring your gifts to the drawing room in twenty minutes. And Hilda?"

His portly housekeeper poked her head in. "Yes, my lord?"

"We're going to need a *lot* more mulled wine."

Jewel raised her cup. "Hear, hear!" she agreed with a grin.

THIRTY-ONE

AMY

*A*MY LOVED presents. Giving them, receiving them, watching others give and receive—she loved all of it. For close to two hours, she'd been basking in the pleasure of watching her loved ones exchange gifts…with no end in sight.

She sipped from her cup of mulled wine, feeling pleasantly relaxed while her niece Elspeth opened yet another present, this one from her mother.

"Oh, my heavens!" Elspeth held up a bow-shaped galant, its gold and jewels flashing in the firelight. "This is lovely!"

"Your Aunty Amy made it," Kendra told her daughter. Toying with the stones on her amber bracelet, she looked to Amy. "I hope you don't mind that I'm passing it along?"

"Of course I don't mind!" Warmth flooded Amy's being, and not just from the wine. She remembered making the delicate brooch—well before she'd met Kendra—setting rubies, emeralds, sapphires, and diamonds in it, seated at her jeweler's bench at Gold-smith & Sons so very many years ago. It seemed a life-time had passed since then, and also since she'd given the galant to Kendra as a thank-you for befriending her after the Great Fire. Kendra hadn't been much older than Elspeth when Amy gave her the galant; the piece was perfect for a young lady, and she was thrilled to see it stay within the family.

Sipping more mulled wine, she looked around the chamber, so pleased to see other pieces she'd made over the years.

Violet was wearing her wedding ring, a large rectangular amethyst with a row of small diamonds flanking each side. When Ford asked Amy to make it, she had been delighted—then even more delighted to see how much Violet loved it.

Complementing her brilliant aquamarine gown, Caithren was wearing the emerald stomacher brooch that Amy had given her as a wedding present. Set with a large oval stone surrounded by diamonds and pearls, it was the first thing Amy made in the workshop Colin built for her at Greystone the year after they'd wed. Seeing it made her remember that and smile.

The jewels in this chamber told the story of her life.

Kendra was wearing the amethyst, diamond, and pearl locket that Colin bought for her birthday so many years before, which Amy had made as well. That had been Colin's first and last visit to Amy's shop—the day the two of them met. So much had happened since then!

The emerald ring on Kendra's hand reminded Amy of her first Christmas as a Chase—and what a magical Christmas that had been. She'd been delighted to celebrate with her new husband's family, and even more delighted to reveal that she was carrying her first child.

On that long-ago Christmas Eve, when Amy gave Kendra that ring, she'd been her only sister-in-law. Now she had three, and she loved them all dearly. Although she'd been raised as an only child, she now found it difficult to imagine life without Kendra, Caithren, and Violet, the sisters of her heart.

Tonight Colin was wearing the cameo cravat pin she gave him before they wed, when she thought she was moving to France and would never see him again. The girl she'd carved into the coral looked very like she had back then: a pert profile with long wavy hair, wearing a little gold wire necklace with a tiny diamond pendant. He also wore the signet ring she'd made for him—well, the second one she'd made, since the first had been taken by a highwayman. He rarely wore any other jewelry, and this occasion was no exception.

Whoever thought she would marry an earl? She still adored him, after all these years. She'd hated being at odds with him—she was so happy the two of them were once again in harmony.

"Why does this always take forever?" Jason asked, pulling out the pocket watch Amy's father made long ago. It had an enamelled face and an open-work lid set with one enormous oval sapphire and eight smaller ones. Following the Great Fire, Amy had given it to Jason as a thank-you gift for letting her stay at his home.

How proud Papa would have been to see a marquess owning his watch, Amy thought now. He'd been a good man, but not a humble one.

Jason flipped the watch open. "It's ten o'clock already, and I swear we're but halfway through."

"There are a lot of us now," Cait reminded him.

"And soon there will be more," Colin added. "Your new little one, plus Jewel will bring Henry."

And maybe Jewel will also bring a little one, Amy thought with a secret smile. A grandchild—she could hardly contain her excitement at the mere possibility.

"For now I've brought these." Jewel began handing out rectangular packages, all wrapped in bright fabrics and tied with pretty ribbons. "You may open my gifts all at once, since they're nearly the same. That will save time and make Uncle Jason happy."

Kendra's daughter Diana accepted her present with a soft smile. She'd always looked up to Jewel, her eldest, most grown-up cousin. "Not yet!" Diana admonished her two younger brothers, who were already untying the ribbons on their gifts. "You have to wait till we all have them!"

When they each had a package, Diana counted —"One, two, three, go!"—and ribbons and fabric went flying.

"A glass box!" she exclaimed. "So pretty! I will treasure it always."

A smile transformed Jewel's face, which Amy thought had looked much too serious lately. "I haven't made leaded-glass boxes since I was a child. I'm so glad you like yours, Diana."

"I shall keep my new galant in it," her older sister, Elspeth, declared. "How did you remember that pink is my favorite color?"

Amy's box featured purple flowers, Cait's had green ones, and the blooms on Kendra's were blue. "She remembered everyone's favorite color," Amy said with a proud grin. Rather than flowers, the men's and boys' boxes featured geometrical designs, also in their favorite colors.

When everyone was finished oohing and aahing over their stained-glass boxes, Amy's son Aidan approached her with a gift. "For you, Mama."

The package was small and wrapped in paper, not

fabric. She untied the slim ribbon and slowly unfolded the paper, revealing a little wooden box. As she opened the lid, she sucked in a breath. "Aidan, these are exquisite!"

The parure of jewels sparkled: a pendant and matching earrings, intended to be worn together. Each piece featured a large oval amethyst surrounded by two dozen round, pear, and marquise-shaped diamonds, arranged in a complicated pattern that managed to look classic and yet thoroughly modern all at once.

For a moment she could only gaze at them. She'd never seen anything like them before. The three matched jewels were gorgeous and unique, in the same way Aidan's talent was unique.

Amy's great-grandpapa had been a master jeweler— her father had always claimed no family member would ever surpass the man's genius and workmanship. *Your talent came from him, you know,* she remembered Papa telling her. *Through the generations. A gift—and an obligation.*

Aidan had inherited that gift. Had he also inherited the obligation?

No.

She quite suddenly knew, with naught but the slimmest thread of guilt-induced doubt: the correct answer was *no.*

Her papa had been wrong, for a gift was a thing

given freely, out of love and generosity. It ought never to be a burden. If she wanted Aidan to find joy in his glorious gift, she had to unburden him.

"I love these," she told him. "I absolutely adore them, and I shall treasure them forever."

"I'm glad to hear that." She watched his jaw set, watched his eyes—so like her own—fill with hostility. "Because they are the last jewels I will ever make."

She let that statement sit there for a moment.

He was clearly expecting a battle.

She was so tired of being defensive.

She'd vowed to her father that Goldsmith & Sons wouldn't die. *The Goldsmith curse,* she'd once called that, so long ago, before any of her children were born. And what had wise Aunt Elizabeth said to her back then?

For God's sake, child, how can you let a promise to a dead man stand in the way of your happiness?

Amy's gaze flicked to her husband. Colin's expression was neither encouraging nor disheartening. He would support her decision either way. After all their months of disagreement, that, in itself, felt like a victory.

Slowly, she sucked in a breath and blew it back out.

"I believe you're a born jeweler," she finally told Aidan gravely. "At only fifteen, a master already, your workmanship unparalleled. There's no telling how far such genius might take you. But it's your life, your choice. Do with it what you wish."

A collective gasp sounded in the room.

Ignoring it, she smiled and reached to give her son the hug he so deserved.

And when her daughter slipped away nearly unnoticed, she didn't give that a second thought.

THIRTY-TWO

KENDRA

*L*AKEFIELD'S MANY clocks had all struck midnight.

It was officially Christmas Day.

All the gifts had been opened. The children were snug in their rooms. The last of the mulled wine was long gone.

And Kendra had never been more ready for bed in her life.

Unfortunately, she and Trick returned to the cottage to find Margaret stripping the very bed she wanted to be in.

At first, Kendra just gaped, confused. She couldn't imagine why this was happening—not *now*, anyway. Why would her maid be changing the sheets in the wee hours on Christmas morning? Especially after they'd been changed as part of the room swap earlier this evening?

"What's happening here?" Trick asked, echoing her thoughts.

"I'm so very sorry, your grace." Margaret looked up, a touch of fear in her eyes. "I spilled a pitcher of water. I vow and swear, I've never been so clumsy—"

"On the bed?" Kendra interrupted in sheer incredulity. Indeed, she could see the washstand pitcher was out of place and empty, but, "On the *bed*?"

The maid looked close to tears. "I was carrying it by, and—"

"It's all right, Margaret," Trick cut in. "We're all clumsy from time to time. Go get some fresh linen. Now, please."

"Yes, your grace." Leaving the wet linen in a heap on the floor, Margaret curtsied, then hurried out.

The moment the door shut, Kendra turned to Trick. "I cannot *believe* that something happened in this chamber, too!"

"Easy, lass. Bide a moment." He kicked the wet heap into a corner. "Margaret will return shortly."

"And then the bed will need to be made, and—"

"Shh." Returning to her, he stopped her rant with a quick kiss. "Compared to all the time we've been waiting, the time to replace sheets will be nothing."

It wouldn't be nothing, but she let him kiss her

again, more deeply. After a moment, she relaxed and felt a familiar warm glow begin spreading through her. Before long she was sighing and happily helping him out of his surcoat.

She kicked off her shoes and sat on the big chest at the foot of the bed to roll off her stockings. He sat beside her and did the same.

A faint moan came through the adjoining wall.

"Do you hear that?" Kendra huffed. "I know her decision made him very happy tonight, but I cannot believe they're together for the *second* time in a matter of hours, while we—"

"Hush, *leannan*." He turned her to face him. "We'll have our chance soon enough. And then they'll be hearing us."

"Oh, no, they won't," she promised, slightly horrified but also amused. When another sound came through the wall, they both laughed. His hands went to detach her stomacher. She leaned close to nuzzle his neck. "Hmm, best to wait. Margaret will be back any moment."

"She's seen you undressed."

"Should we go any further, I'll be more than undressed…"

A knock came at the door. "Your graces?"

"Told you so," Kendra muttered as Trick strode over to open it.

Margaret came in, carrying what looked to be a few threadbare towels. "I'm so very sorry—" she started.

"Where are the linens?" Kendra all but shrieked, her newfound good humor shattered.

Margaret's blue eyes looked huge, the tears that had threatened earlier welling. "The laundress has gone to bed for the night, and the extra sets of bedding were used yesterday to fix the cheese stench and then earlier today after the cats got into your room. There are so many people in the house, more people than ever before, and I woke the housekeeper, but she told me there's simply no more clean bedding. No good towels, either, but I brought these old—"

"Well, then, let's use them," Kendra snapped, snatching one of them from the girl's hands.

Trick grabbed another, and the three of them laid all the old towels end to end—covering perhaps one-third of the big featherbed.

"This is it?" Kendra asked bleakly, suddenly feeling all worn out. "There's no more clean linen anywhere?"

A single tear made its way down Margaret's cheek as she shook her head sorrowfully. "I'm so sorry, your grace. So, so sorry I spilled—"

"Everyone makes mistakes," Trick broke in. "Don't be so hard on yourself," he added soothingly.

Kendra felt far from soothed. Frustration and fatigue were battling inside her. "Apparently *our* mistake was expecting even a moment of peace at Christmas," she grumbled with an elaborate sigh.

She considered sleeping on the bare tick, but rejected that thought immediately. It was stuffed with down and feathers that would poke her all night without linens to cover it.

"We'll sleep in the room Cas and Pol are sharing, since it has two beds," she decided dejectedly. "That will be all, Margaret. Happy Christmas."

"H-happy Christmas to you, your grace," Margaret said through a sniffle as she left the room.

Kendra just stood there barefoot for a moment, listening to the maid blow her nose in the corridor before making her way up the stairs to the attic.

THIRTY-THREE

JEWEL

FROM THE FAR end of the corridor, Jewel watched Margaret blow her nose and tuck the handkerchief back into her sleeve. Then the maid squared her shoulders and came running (or was that skipping?), softly giggling all the way.

"It went all right, then?" Jewel asked when Margaret reached her.

"It went splendidly, my lady." A wide smile spread on the girl's face. "Is it terrible of me to think this has been fun?"

"I certainly hope not." Jewel smiled in return. "Because if you're terrible, I'm worse."

THIRTY-FOUR

KENDRA

ONCE THE MAID'S footsteps had faded, Kendra turned to Trick. "*I* should be the one crying, not Margaret."

"Ah, lassie, it's not bad enough to warrant tears from either of you," he replied and wrapped her in a hug that was clearly meant to be consoling.

But she couldn't help turning her face up for a kiss.

She wanted him so badly.

Unsurprisingly, it wasn't long before the kisses turned into more. Kendra inhaled Trick's oh-so-familiar sandalwood scent and fairly melted into his arms. When his hands went to detach her stomacher again, she didn't stop him. As he unlaced her bodice beneath it, a ripple of excitement shot through her.

"Maybe we should try the bed without linens," she murmured. "We can cover it with blankets. There were extras in the chest in the other chamber."

Leaving her dress gaping open, she went back to the chest at the foot of the bed. And lifted the heavy lid. And found…

Nothing.

The chest was empty.

She dropped the lid with a *bang*. "I was sure there would be blankets in here." The ones she'd seen in the other room had been wool and would have been itchy, but that was better than being poked.

He came closer and drew her bodice off her shoulder, kissing the skin he'd bared. "Maybe we can get them from our old chamber."

Another faint moan sounded from next door. "I'm not interrupting *that*. Where is the counterpane, anyway?" She glanced at the soggy pile in the corner. "It's not there."

He was kissing his way up her neck, making her shiver—and not from the cold. "Margaret might have taken it from the room before we arrived." His words tickled warmly against her throat. "It would have been even wetter than the sheets."

"Perhaps," she said with a distracted sigh. "The pillows are gone, too. I suppose everything on top would have been wetter. What now?"

He lifted his head and scanned the fancy red brocade bed hangings.

"No," she said with a choked laugh. "They're far too high to detach. And we can't destroy Violet's lovely new guest room—she dressed this bed so beautifully."

"For all the good it's done us." Though the sentiment was negative, his tone sounded much less defeated than she felt. "Hell, *leannan*, are you going to let a missing sheet or blanket stop us?"

If he was still hopeful, perhaps she should be, too. "Maybe we don't need a covering."

Maybe she wouldn't get poked as much as she feared.

"That's my lass." Wasting no time, he threw off his remaining clothes and backed her toward the bed, aiming for the side where the towels were laid out. When she felt the feather tick behind her, she sank onto it, reaching to pull him down with her.

"Ugh!" she exclaimed, bounding back up. She hadn't been poked. Instead she'd got soaked. "How many pitchers of water did she spill on here? Five?"

Trick scooped up the towels and began dabbing at the mattress. For all of ten seconds. "The bed is drenched," he said, stating the obvious. "We will have to wait for it to dry naturally."

"That could take all night!"

"And half of tomorrow as well," Trick agreed.

"We'll be on our way home by then," Kendra wailed. "This is so unfair!"

"Hush, lassie. People are sleeping in here."

"Clearly they aren't," she said, rolling her eyes toward the other chamber. Disgusted, she headed to the wardrobe, pulling her dress off as she went. "Let me swap this wet gown for a nightgown, then we'll head down to Cas and Pol's room."

"Kendra…"

Shivering in just her damp chemise, she turned back to face him in all his aroused glory. Her breath caught in her throat.

She swallowed hard. "Yes?"

"You're giving up?"

"You're not?" she asked, incredulous.

For a moment, he just gazed at her, commanding her attention.

A beat of silence passed between them. The pit of her stomach began tingling.

"There's no smelly cheese in here," he said at last. "We're not overwhelmingly sleepy. The door is intact. I'm not seeing any cats. And I want you," he continued, his voice taking on that tinge of a Scottish accent she heard when he got emotional. "And I'm thinking you want me."

She found herself caught in his fathomless amber eyes. "I do," she breathed.

"Then why should we give up?"

"The bed is soaked."

"Since when do we need a bed?" he asked in a tone that sent her back to a long-ago day in Scotland, to an ancient dungeon deep in the earth. Like in a dream, she remembered him lifting her, wrapping her legs around his middle, a rough stone wall against her back...

She wasn't sure whether the sound she made was a gasp or a snigger. "I'm not twenty-three anymore. And there's no free wall space in here."

She watched his gaze sweep the room—the big window, the fireplace, the many pieces of heavy carved furniture—before lingering on the small parquet table and its two plush chairs.

Now she sniggered for real. "I'm not making love on one of Violet's brand-new velvet chairs. We don't even have a blanket to cover it. And don't even *think* about the table," she added, figuring she was reading his mind. "It's on a pedestal. It will tilt."

That deterred him for but a moment. "There's the floor," he pointed out. "That won't tilt."

And before she knew what was happening, he was lowering her to it.

Slightly skeptical, she let herself sink to the polished wood. And when he came down beside her, she turned to face him and let him kiss her senseless.

Well, not quite senseless.

Before long she sensed her hip was hurting. A lot.

218 | LAUREN ROYAL

The floor was hard, her thin chemise was useless as padding, and they didn't have so much as a blanket.

Her shoulder was hurting, too. And the side of her knee. And her elbow.

With no pillow, her neck was bent awkwardly and beginning to ache.

She'd been right to be skeptical, damn it. Reluctantly, she broke the kiss.

"I'm too old for this," she grumbled, pulling away and pushing herself to a sitting position. "I give up." Both figuratively and literally, she threw up her hands. "I officially give up."

Trick's only response was a groan. He rolled onto his back and flung an arm over his eyes. Then he just lay there, still and silent.

She wouldn't let her gaze move down his body. She wouldn't. Instead, with more difficulty than she wanted to admit—even to herself—she raised her uncooperative forty-three-year-old bones and went to the wardrobe.

They remained silent while she changed into her thickest nightgown. Silent while she grabbed his robe and tossed it on top of him. Silent while she snatched up a candle and headed out of the chamber.

Silent while he followed her downstairs and into their sons' room.

Silent while she tried and failed to wake Cas, then woke Pol and helped him stumble sleepily into his brother's bed.

She and Trick crawled into the vacated bed, she in her nightgown, he in his robe. She blew out the candle. The single bed was narrow, and they didn't fit well lying flat, so she turned on her side and snuggled into him. He snaked an arm over her, pulling her even closer.

She listened to the twins' breathing, which synchronized as they settled back into sound sleep. Consciously relaxing, she breathed along with them.

In...out.

In...out.

Just as she was about to nod off, Trick broke the silence with a whisper. "This bed is much softer than the floor, is it not?"

Disappointed, defeated, and drained, she could muster only a vague noise of agreement.

He squeezed her tighter. "Feels good."

"Hmm," she murmured sleepily.

His fingers slipped out from under her and grabbed a handful of her nightgown. He began bunching it, pulling it up.

Horrified, she flipped to face him—never mind that she couldn't see him in the dark. "What on earth," she whispered fiercely, "do you think you are doing?"

"Are you serious?" he whispered in a cadence that suggested she must be addlepated. "What we've been trying to do for three days straight."

"Are you insane?" she returned. "We've got two thirteen-year-olds five feet from us!"

"They're sleeping."

"You think that will last?"

"It's pitch black in here. They won't see anything."

"I suppose you think they won't hear anything as well?" Somehow she managed to whisper a snort. "I thought I'd made it clear I've given up. I'm going to sleep. I suggest you do the same."

She turned her back on him again. He snaked his arm around her again. She laced her fingers with his, effectively stopping them from doing anything.

And then she *did* go to sleep.

❄

*W*HAT FELT like five minutes later (but might have been an hour), Trick nuzzled her neck. "I have an idea," he whispered warm in her ear.

"Hmm?"

"The ducal carriage is very plush…"

"I just fell asleep." She blinked herself half-awake. "The coach house is across two courtyards. And it's freezing out there."

"It could be hailing cannonballs, for all I care." She felt him roll to sit, then rise. She heard him walk to the door and open it, admitting a little light from the common room's fireplace. In the faint glow, she watched him jerk his robe's sash tighter. "I'll be right back," he whispered.

She closed her eyes and willed herself back to sleep. Or at least she *tried* to will herself back to sleep. Butterflies in her stomach seemed to be keeping her awake, not to mention a new yet persistent tingling between her legs.

He returned with shoes for her, boots for himself, and their two cloaks. "We could have used these cloaks for the floor," he murmured with some measure of disgust at himself. "What was I thinking?"

"You weren't. Neither of us were. And the carriage will be more comfortable anyway," she added, warming to the idea as her body anticipated what would happen in that carriage.

Out in the common room, they donned their footwear and wrapped themselves in their cloaks. Trick lit a torch from the fireplace. They crept from the cottage as quietly as possible, then ran for it, crossing the two snowy courtyards in record time.

They banged into the coach house and shoved the giant doors shut behind them before dissolving into uncontrollable laughter. Kendra felt like a sixteen-year-old sneaking out to attend a forbidden ball.

Until Trick grabbed her with one arm, still holding the torch with the other, and met her lips for a desperate kiss.

Then she felt like a long-married woman.

A *deprived* long-married woman.

She wound her arms around his neck and pressed herself close. With calculated skill, he kissed her breathless. When he broke the kiss, she stared at him helplessly. Her lips tingled. She fought to catch her breath, making white puffs in the coach house's chilly air.

Without a word between them, they made their way to the ducal carriage. Trick leaned inside to light both lamps, then secured the torch to the coach house wall while she climbed up and dropped bonelessly to one of the wide, plush seats.

He sat himself across from her, pulling the door closed to hold in their warmth. They tugged off their shoes and shucked off their cloaks. Then they just gazed at each other for a long, tension-filled moment, until he offered a hand to draw her over to him.

Facing him, she straddled his legs. His lips went to hers immediately, the kiss deepening while he reached beneath her nightgown to arrange her knees on the soft, thickly padded bench, then tucked the carriage's velvet pillows around them.

Her heart beat double-time in the cushioned stillness. His fingers were warm, and so was his breath, flavored with the faintest trace of the mulled wine he'd sipped earlier. A dizzying cloud of his sandalwood scent surrounded her. She found herself stunned by how much she'd missed him.

By how much she'd missed *this*.

When he broke the kiss, she burrowed into his neck. "I forbid you to ever leave me again," she murmured against his skin.

"God forbid I ever have to." He took her face between his hands. "I wanted you every day, *leannan*, every hour, sometimes every minute."

He kissed her again, gently, strengthening the stirrings in her belly that had begun in the twins' room. As she strained closer, a low hum of satisfaction vibrated from his throat and spread all through her. The kiss turned hot and needy, his tongue sweeping into her mouth, meeting hers with a thrilling urgency. She ran her own tongue across the tiny chipped corner of his front tooth. Craving his solid warmth, she fought with the tie on his robe until she managed to open it and slip her hands inside, reveling in the feel of his skin and hard muscles against her questing palms.

When at last they came up for air, she leaned back in his embrace, gazing up into his seductive amber eyes. The faint golden stubble on his chin glistened in the lamplight. She rested her hands against his chest. Beneath her fingertips, the beat of his heart matched hers.

He was the center of her world. The only man she had ever loved.

She wrapped her arms around his neck and threaded her fingers in his silky, straight hair. He leaned closer to plant little kisses on her cheeks, her nose, her forehead, the sensitive hollow of her neck. He lingered there, suckling gently while his hands went to work lifting her nightgown. He yanked it over her head, releasing a frustrated laugh when her arms tangled in the full-blown sleeves.

Finally it was gone, and she plastered herself against him, skin to skin. Closing her eyes, she threw back her head and surrendered herself to the sensations. Ah, the give and the take, the heat and the scent, the pure pleasure of his bareness touching hers. She'd missed this.

She'd *so* missed this.

Her senses were spinning, and an urgency was building deep inside her, more swiftly than ever before in her memory. Her eyes still shut, she inched closer, feeling a hot stab of desire where her body nearly met his.

"Oh, God, Trick." Dear heavens, he was right there, almost inside her. She wanted him there, filling her where she ached. When he ran his hands down her shoulders and around to cup her breasts, she placed her own hands over them. "Next time," she murmured blindly against his lips. "I cannot wait."

He hesitated. Her heart pounded, her breath coming ragged and uneven. Every fiber of her being ached for him inside her, screamed for release.

"Now," she demanded breathlessly.

"Look at me, lass."

Her eyes fluttered open. Beneath his shining gold

hair, his eyes caught and held her gaze. She'd never seen anything so intense and compelling in her life. "I want you," she breathed.

"God," he said huskily, "how I dreamed of this, all the time I was gone."

"*Now*," she demanded again.

Finally, finally, his hands moved to her waist. Finally, finally he lifted her, then guided her back down, slowly, slowly, still holding her gaze captive as his hands held her steady. She felt herself opening, welcoming his warmth into hers.

As she settled against him, she felt a jolt, a flood of excitement that made her tremble, and when they moved together, a heavenly friction that made her gasp. Had anything ever felt so good as physical love long denied?

She'd done this more than a thousand times. But this time felt new. As their tempo quickened, she felt a delicious throbbing, and she couldn't tell if it was hers or his. Then it grew, until she knew it belonged to them both. Until she felt him pulsing within her and responded in a burst of exquisite glory.

It seemed a long while before she could think straight, before Trick placed one last cherishing kiss on her lips.

"Welcome home," she whispered.

THIRTY-FIVE

JEWEL

*E*AGER TO GET outdoors for one last snowball fight, the younger generation was rushing through Aunty Violet's much-anticipated Christmas breakfast when a footman stepped into the room.

"Pray pardon, Lord Lakefield," he said. "A messenger is wishing to speak with you."

Uncle Ford rose and left the chamber.

Jewel thought nothing of it. While her cousins resumed shoveling food into their mouths and the rest of the family continued chattering, she savored a bite of panperdy. Breakfast was proving even more delicious than promised, especially this fine manchet bread fried in eggs and spices. More to the point, she felt cheerful and full of confidence this morning.

Back to feeling like herself at last.

As she'd climbed into bed last night, a tiny part of her had wondered if perhaps the mulled wine had been speaking when *"I've decided to accept"* came out of her mouth. But she'd awakened completely sober and free of regret.

She'd triumphed over Rowan, and she'd made her decision, and life was grand. If the wine had helped her do all that, perhaps she ought to consider drinking more often.

"I have news," Uncle Ford announced upon his return. Looking a bit stunned, he plopped back onto his chair. "King James fled the country two days ago. It's over. William and Mary will be our next king and queen."

"No war," Hugh said with what sounded to Jewel like a disappointed sigh.

"What a wonderful Christmas gift!" Mama exclaimed.

"Thank God," Aunty Violet breathed. "A relatively peaceful revolution. But will we, the people, gain more power? Will our new monarchs sign a Bill of Rights?"

Uncle Jason's jaw set with resolve. "If we Chases have anything to say about it, they will."

A great cheer went up. It was a wonderful Christmas gift indeed, and soon they would usher in a glorious new year, with no threat of war.

The chatter resumed in an ebullient tone. Feeling

even more lighthearted than before, Jewel toyed with her panperdy while her cousins asked to be excused one after another in a comically clockwork fashion.

"Don't you want to join them?" Mama asked when she was the only cousin remaining at the table. "The thirteen of you are all together so rarely."

Jewel shrugged. "I'm not done eating. And childish snow play is not appealing to me this morning. I'm twenty-one and all but betrothed, after all."

"Ah, I see," Mama said with a delighted smile that convinced Jewel she had fallen for her excuse.

In truth, Jewel wondered if she'd *ever* feel too old for snow play, for, betrothed or not, she would have thoroughly enjoyed pelting her kin with snowballs were she not determined to stay indoors. But the breakfast table offered an even better entertainment, one she'd been looking forward to all morning: the look on Aunty Kendra's and Uncle Trick's faces when they learned about her father's prank.

And even more so: The look on Papa's face when he learned of *her* involvement.

All of which seemed imminent now that the children had all left, if she could judge by the look in Papa's eyes...

"Did you enjoy a pleasant holiday, Kendra?" he asked between bites of buttered eggs.

"Very much so." Aunty Kendra sipped from her

tankard of warm chocolate. "Why do you ask? Haven't we all had a pleasant holiday?"

He focused on cutting a bite of bacon. "I was just wondering if you might have found the past two days a mite"—he looked up and straight at her—"frustrating."

Over the tankard's rim, she slanted him a puzzled glance. "And why would you wonder that?"

"Perhaps because I was keeping you and your husband apart," he suggested with a raise of one devilish black brow.

"What?" Aunty Kendra's tankard hit the table. "*What* did you just say?"

Uncle Trick's eyes narrowed. "You mean the putrid cheese, the broken hinges, the damned cats—"

"All of it," Papa cut in proudly. "Don't forget the posset laced with valerian—"

"Wait," Aunty Cait interrupted. "You told me the valerian was for Aidan."

Papa's expression was all innocence. "I did save some for Aidan. Happily, he no longer needs it."

"What's valerian?" Aunty Violet asked.

"A dried root." Aunty Cait wasn't one for rolling her eyes, but Jewel thought she looked on the verge of it. "Ground up and mixed into a drink, a small pinch can often help one sleep."

"Help?" Uncle Trick scoffed. "Those drinks rendered us dead to the world for twelve hours and counting.

Had Margaret not awakened us, we might *still* be sleeping."

"Margaret?" Aunty Kendra murmured in a contemplative tone. "Margaret…"

Jewel crossed her fingers beneath the table, hoping the maid wouldn't find herself in trouble.

"Margaret." Aunty Kendra shot Papa an accusatory glare. "My maid Margaret brought us those drinks, not you."

Papa shrugged. "Your maid Margaret might have done so at my direction."

"Might have?" Her eyes widened. "What is that supposed to mean? Margaret is the most loyal—"

"Margaret was bribed," Jewel piped up, unable to help herself.

Her father's gaze snapped to her. "How would *you* know that?"

She flipped her long hair over her shoulder. "I might have been helping Margaret."

A mix of astonishment and pride filled his eyes. "How the hell did *that* happen?"

"You know how much I enjoy a good prank," she said blithely while her insides danced with delight. "I figured out what you and Margaret were doing and wanted in."

"You figured it out, yet they didn't," he crowed, a flick of one hand indicating his sister and Uncle Trick. "That's my girl."

Wait till he hears the rest, Jewel thought with a secret smile.

Aunty Kendra speared another sugary bite. "You're not as smart as you think you are, Colin Chase."

"No?"

"The wet bed didn't keep us apart."

"What wet bed?" Papa's puzzled frown made Jewel stifle a giggle. "What do you mean?"

"You know what I mean," Kendra said without elaborating further. "Note that it didn't work, which makes your prank an unqualified failure, would you not agree?"

The pout on Papa's face would have better fit a toddling two-year-old. "*What* wet bed?"

Jewel couldn't draw it out any longer. "Margaret and I spilled water on their bed last night." The grin she'd been hiding broke free. "A *lot* of water. And we stole all their blankets and pillows."

"I was finished!" he burst out.

She feigned a nonchalant shrug. "I wasn't."

While Papa's mouth hung open, Kendra pointed a forkful of sugared pan cakes at him. "I cannot believe you managed to bribe that sweet girl."

He didn't look the least bit sorry—for bribing Aunty Kendra's maid, anyway. "Everyone has a price," he informed her.

"What was hers?"

"Twenty pounds," Jewel said. "But I think we should

make him give her thirty, so she can marry her love immediately."

Aunty Kendra dropped the fork. "Margaret has a love?"

"A grand love, from what she's told me. His name is Richard, and he's a footman at Foxbow Manor," Jewel began, then regaled them with Margaret's sad tale.

Kendra remained rapt throughout the whole story. "No wonder Margaret has been so upset about leaving Amberley," she said once Jewel had finished. "That would also mean leaving her young man." She turned to Jewel's father. "Give me thirty pounds."

"If you insist," he said with a mock sigh. He pulled out his heavy pouch and counted out twenty-nine gold guineas, each worth a pound and a shilling, then shoved them toward her on the table. "Keep the change."

"Margaret will keep the change—what little will be left after settling the debt with Richard's odious employers." She looked to Jewel. "I understand you're in need of a maid. What do you think of Margaret?"

"I like her." In fact, Jewel more than liked her—she felt a kinship with Margaret, having teamed up with her to play the prank. Lydia had never been willing to help her play pranks. "But surely you wouldn't dismiss her over a prank?"

"Of course not. She's a lovely girl and a fine maid. It's just that I feel she's ready to go out in the world, and I'd like to train another girl from the orphanage."

"I'd be pleased to have Margaret for my maid," Jewel said. "And Papa will also hire her love, so the two of them can marry and live together."

"I will?" her father said.

"You will. At least until I'm wed, at which point Henry will hire them both."

He only grunted.

"She always has had you wrapped around her little finger," Mama pointed out to him as though Jewel weren't there. "Is it any surprise she thinks she'll be able to control her husband as easily?"

"I wish the young man luck," Papa said dryly.

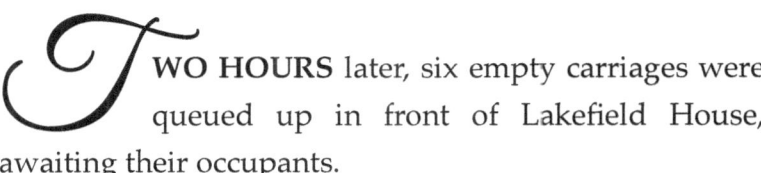

WO HOURS later, six empty carriages were queued up in front of Lakefield House, awaiting their occupants.

Uncle Jason's family had left immediately after breakfast, anxious to attend to their annual Cainewood community Christmas. The rest of the family were still inside the house, sorting out last-minute details for their journeys home. Well, except for Uncle Ford and Aunty Violet, who were preparing to travel the mile to Trentingham for their Ashcroft holiday gathering, a week-long family tradition that would last till the new year.

Jewel left the house first, in search of Margaret. She'd been told she could find her directing the placement of

Aunty Kendra's luggage on Amberley's baggage cart, and it looked as though she'd just finished.

When Margaret saw her approach, her big blue eyes filled with tears again.

Jewel hoped they were happy tears. "Did my aunt tell you the news?"

"Oh, my lady," Margaret gushed, "I'll be forever grateful. For my new position, for your father's offer to employ Richard, and especially for the extra funds that will free the two of us to wed. Her grace told me you'd suggested that. It all feels like a Christmas miracle."

"I'm so glad you're pleased," Jewel told her. "Happy Christmas. And my thanks for your assistance with our, um…escapades."

The tears disappeared, and a little laugh bubbled up in their stead. "Anytime, my lady. I'd enjoy more escapades. You've only to ask."

"I'll be asking, I assure you." Jewel could tell they would get on like a house on fire. Overcome with good Christmas feelings, she impulsively gave her new maid a hug.

The rest of the family began straggling outdoors, Papa and Aunty Kendra in the lead.

"Your grace?" Margaret bobbed a curtsy to get Aunty Kendra's attention. "Is there anything else you need?"

"I believe that's it. Run along and fetch your own things." Aunty Kendra looked to Papa. "Wait till Friday to send a carriage for Margaret and her love, will you? That will give them time to settle their debt while I select a new maid from the orphanage."

"Will do," he said, opening their carriage door to put Mama's new book inside.

Five cats bounded out.

"What the devil?"

"Is there a problem?" Aunty Kendra asked sweetly.

Too sweetly.

He stuck his head inside and waved the book to shoo one last cat from the compartment. "How did these creatures get in here?"

Jewel was surprised to find herself quicker on the uptake than her father.

"How should I know?" Aunty Kendra asked him with a shrug. "But there's no reason to be upset about it. It's not as though cats make you sneeze."

"Lord Greystone, we have a mishap," Papa's man Benchley called out, approaching with two footmen carrying his trunk. "The hinges on this seem to be malfunctioning."

Jewel stifled a laugh.

Papa frowned. "In what way?"

"Oh, my," Aunty Kendra said although he hadn't been asking her. "I'm sure I don't know how that happened, either."

Perhaps finally catching on, he shot her a suspicious glance before beckoning to the footmen. "Let me see."

The two men lowered the trunk to the graveled drive. Papa bent and threw open the lid to investigate—only to watch it fly off. It landed with a *bang* and a spray of tiny gray stones, which thankfully missed everyone.

Jewel burst out laughing.

"I should have guessed the pins would be missing," Papa announced with a good-natured snort, then straightened and backed up, coughing. Or maybe choking. "God's blood," he grated out.

Aunty Kendra grinned. "Problem, Colin? A noxious scent, perhaps? Could there be…cheese in your trunk?" She lifted one of his shirts with two fingertips, holding it as far from herself as possible. Smeared with cheese, it dripped copiously onto the gravel. "Oh, and it seems a pitcher of water may have ended up in your trunk too, poor you. Or two or three pitchers. Or maybe four."

The rest of the family dissolved in laughter a moment after Papa did. "The water was *her* fault," he chortled, indicating Jewel.

"I'll get her another time," Kendra said with a wave of her free hand. She dropped the shirt back in the trunk, where it landed with a splash. "I win."

"No," he declared between chuckles, "you lose. You failed to slip me some valerian. And now you're leaving."

"The day's not over yet," she shot back with an arch smile. "Just remember the next time you're given something to eat or drink: everyone has a price."

Aunty Kendra winked at Jewel, and Jewel grinned back, unworried about any retribution from her aunt at all.

"Happy Christmas, dear brother," Aunty Kendra said with all good humor. Then she glanced around before adding, "Happy Christmas to all my dear family!"

"Happy Christmas!" fifteen Chases returned in unison, Jewel among them.

What a Christmas this had turned out to be, she mused with a satisfied sigh. As much as her last few days had been dominated by her big decision, they had also been filled with love and joy, fun and laughter. And now she had her wedding and Aunty Caithren's new baby to look forward to before next Christmas at Cainewood. And a whole new life ahead of her.

She hugged herself, thinking she had never been happier.

Surrounded by her loving family, she was certain 1689 was going to be her best year yet, the year she'd see all her hopes and dreams fulfilled.

Nothing—and no one—would stand in her way.

AUTHOR'S NOTE

Dear Reader,

When King Charles II died in 1685 without a legitimate heir, his brother King James II took the throne. This was a time when relations between Catholics and Protestants were tense. James was Catholic and also had close ties with France, a connection that concerned many citizens. But James's daughter Mary, a Protestant, was the rightful heir to the throne, which kept things in check for a while.

In 1687, King James formally dissolved Parliament and attempted to create a new Parliament that would support him unconditionally, angering much of the aristocracy. Then, in June 1688, his son James Francis Edward Stuart was born, and he announced that the baby would be raised Catholic. This changed the line of succession. Many feared a Catholic dynasty was imminent, and this is when whispers of a revolt began.

Opponents of the king issued an invitation to Mary's husband, William of Orange, a Dutch prince and nephew of James (yup, Mary wed her first cousin), pledging their allegiance if he invaded England. William assembled an impressive armada and arrived in November 1688. Seeing the writing on the wall, King James fled the country on December 23 of that same year—the year *A Chase Family Christmas* takes place.

Today this event is called the Glorious Revolution, and it marked a big step in the shift of power from the monarchy to Parliament, ultimately changing how England was governed. Parliament granted the crown jointly to William and Mary in exchange for them signing a Bill of Rights. The monarchy in England would never hold absolute power again.

To see William and Mary's coronation, watch for my next book, which will continue Jewel's story!

Of course Ford Chase didn't invent modern ice skates, any more than he invented frames to hold spectacles on the face or the first watch with a minute hand (even though I had him design both of those things in his own book, *Never Doubt a Viscount*).

Ice skates have been around for many millennium. The oldest pair of ice skates found so far, at the bottom of a lake in northern Europe, are estimated to have been worn in about 3000 B.C.

The earliest skates were made from animal bone, with holes drilled in each end and leather straps to tie the skates to skaters' shoes. In the 14th century, the Dutch developed wooden platform skates with iron runners on the bottom. In the 15th century, they refined the design to make the blade double-edged, like the skate blades we use today.

Until the 17th century, ice skating was used mostly for transportation along frozen rivers and canals. While in exile, however, young King Charles II tried ice skating in Holland and thought it a fun sport. In exile with him, this is when my Chase family would have begun skating.

When Charles regained his throne, he introduced skating for sport to England. Historians believe that the British were the first to use the blades of their skates to make tracings and drawings on the ice, and in 1763, England hosted the first official ice skating competition.

As for skates that feature a clamping mechanism, that inventor was probably Pennsylvanian E.V. Bushnell in 1848, or else John Forbes, a young Scottish immigrant to Canada in the 1860s. American skater Jackson Haines added the first toe pick to skates around 1870, which made jumps possible for the first time. If Ford Chase had really lived more than 150 years earlier, could he have been brilliant enough to invent skates that featured toe picks and clamped to shoes? I like to think so!

In the scene where Jason returns to Cait, he refers to

a Gypsy fortune-teller they met in their own book. While I'm aware that the word "Gypsy" is often considered a pejorative term these days, I chose to use it for historical accuracy, because no other words existed in the English language that my characters could call the Romani people at that time. As the term wasn't considered derogatory in the 1680s, I hope you will consider my choice as respectful as it was intended.

Ford and Violet's home was inspired by a real house called Snowshill Manor. Taking literary license, I've placed Lakefield House on the bank of the Thames near Windsor, though Snowshill is actually in the Cotswolds.

Snowshill was owned by Winchcombe Abbey from the year 821 until the reign of Henry VIII in the 16th century, when, with the dissolution of the monasteries, it passed to the Crown. Thereafter Snowshill had many owners and tenants, until 1919, when a man named Charles Paget Wade returned from the First World War and found it for sale.

The house was derelict, and the garden was an overgrown jumble of weeds with a sundial, all of which play a part in Ford's book, *Never Doubt a Viscount*, where Ford restores everything much as Wade did in real life. Wade removed the plaster ceilings, moved partitions back to their original places, unblocked fireplaces, and fit Tudor paneling to many of the rooms to recapture the original atmosphere. He scorned the use of electricity and modern conveniences, so the house appears today much as it would have during Ford's time.

Wade never lived in the house. Instead he lived in the adjacent Priest's House (the "cottage" in this book) and used the main house to showcase his amazing collection of everyday and curious objects, literally thousands of items including musical instruments, clocks, toys, weavers' and spinners' tools, and Japanese armor. He also accumulated a massive assortment of bicycles, which are currently displayed in the space I used as Ford's laboratory.

The home is now owned by the National Trust and open April through October. If you're ever in the Cotswolds, I recommend a visit!

I hope you enjoyed *A Chase Family Christmas*! If you love holiday romances, look for *A Secret Christmas*, where Chrystabel and Joseph Ashcroft meet and fall in love. And if you've read the whole Chase Family Series, check out *Tempt Me at Midnight*, which features descendants of the Chases many years later, in the Regency era. Please read on for excerpts as well as more bonus material!

Always,

Lauren

Read on for an excerpt from

A Secret
Christmas

Book 8 of the
Chase Family Series
by Lauren Royal

Christmas has been outlawed by the new Commonwealth government—but that won't stop Lady Chrystabel Trevor from embracing the holiday spirit. When she finds herself snowed in with handsome and intriguing Joseph Ashcroft, the Viscount Tremayne, merrymaking leads to mayhem. In a time of fear and oppression, can the magic of Christmas bring two hearts together?

Grosmont Grange, England
December 20, 1651

LADY CHRYSTABEL Trevor adored Christmas.

Or at least she had until this year.

She frowned as her sap-sticky hands wove yet another wreath from the greenery she and her younger sister had collected. "Just five more days," she said, thinking of all the decorating they still had to do.

Arabel meticulously measured two loops of red ribbon. "But just four days until Christmas Eve."

"Yes, and we have to be ready by Christmas Eve." Chrystabel sighed as she eyed the enormous pile of boughs they'd cut and trimmed. "I cannot believe how long it took to make the garlands. This isn't easy alone."

"You're not alone, Chrystabel." Arabel sounded

sweetly sympathetic. "I'm still here. Matthew's still here."

"Martha and Cecily aren't here." Martha and Cecily were their older sisters. "And neither is Mother." Not that Mother had helped her girls prepare for Christmas, anyway. She'd always been a rather uninvolved parent, leaving her children to be raised by nursemaids. But this was their first Christmas without her, and having her home and not participating had been better than not having her with them at all. "It makes me sad that we never see her."

"Just pretend she's dead," Arabel suggested airily.

Arabel said everything airily. Pretty, seventeen-year-old Arabel was dark-haired and dark-eyed and statuesque—like Chrystabel and the rest of the Trevors—and she was the happiest person Chrystabel knew. Nothing ruffled her. She could find the good side of anything.

Unabated cheerfulness like that set Chrystabel's teeth on edge.

"Mother is not dead," she pointed out unnecessarily. "I could forgive her if she were dead." Their father had died, after all—fighting for the king in the Civil War—and Chrystabel had never blamed *him* for leaving them. Death was sad but normal.

But there was nothing normal about being alive and not even an hour's ride away—and ignoring your own children.

Especially at Christmas.

Chrystabel set her jaw. "I will never forgive her for marrying that...*that* man."

That man was the Marquess of Bath, and he had no interest in the grown children of his second wife. The sorry and shocking thing was that Mother seemed similarly disinclined to spend time with her first family. She was too busy with her new husband and his children that she was raising. *Raising.* Even though she'd barely deigned to notice Chrystabel and her brother and three sisters—the five children she'd given birth to—all the years they were growing up.

"You cannot let Mother's selfishness ruin our Christmas," Arabel chided. "We're not children anymore. Let it go. I have. Martha and Cecily have."

"Martha and Cecily are married with children of their own. They don't need a mother anymore."

"For heaven's sake, Chrys, you're nineteen years old—you don't need a mother anymore, either." Arabel handed her a perfect red bow. "Here. Attach it, and that's one more wreath finished."

"Still twelve more to make," Chrystabel said with a sigh.

Arabel's laugh sounded suspiciously like a snort. "You're the one who insists upon decorating this entire, huge house."

Arabel was right about that—and more. Chrystabel knew she needed to dispense with the anger she felt toward their mother. It served no purpose. She would take a lesson from her less-than-ideal childhood: When she had her own family, she would do better.

Right then and there, she determined to do better.

"Look." For once, Arabel wore a frown. She motioned out the window. "Soldiers. Parliamentarian soldiers."

Hearing hoofbeats approach down Grosmont Grange's long, icy, hard-packed drive, Chrystabel dragged her thoughts from her mother to follow her sister's gaze. Sure enough, the horsemen wore breastplates over buff leather coats, with lobster-tailed pot helmets on their heads. Oliver Cromwell's Dragoons.

They couldn't be bringing good news to a Royalist family.

Since the war had ended in September, the formerly fighting Dragoons were now roaming the countryside, enforcing Cromwell's strict Puritanical laws: no music, no dancing, no theater, no sports, no swearing, no drinking, no gaming…no Christmas.

No Christmas!

"They mean to catch us preparing for Christmas!" Chrystabel ran from the chamber and down the corridor to her brother's study. "Matthew, open up!" Without waiting, she pushed open the door and burst inside. "Dragoons! Here to catch us celebrating Christmas!"

Arabel had already scooped up as much greenery as

she could carry and was racing past the open door. "Where should we put it?" she called.

"Under your bed, then go back for more—we'll put it under mine!" Chrystabel turned back to Matthew. "We'll hide everything. You answer the door when they arrive."

It took three trips to and from the drawing room to hide all the Christmas evidence beneath their two beds. Once the sisters were finished, they shut the door to Chrystabel's room and plopped onto the mattress side by side, pretending to be reading books.

"Surely they won't look under our beds," Arabel whispered in her usual cheerful manner.

"We can hope not," Chrystabel muttered back.

Time passed while she listened to her own heartbeat and reread the same paragraph thirteen times.

"I don't hear anyone searching the house," Arabel said. "And they were wearing heavy boots."

Chrystabel shrugged. "As you recently pointed out, it's a big house. They'll get here."

They both jumped when a sharp knock came at the door.

Chrystabel steeled herself. "Enter if you must."

"I must," their brother said as the door swung open.

"Matthew! Are they gone?"

"They are." He suddenly looked older than his twenty-five years. His handsome face appeared ashen. For the first time, he looked like the Earl of Grosmont to her, not just her big brother who unfortunately had inherited early.

"Why did they not search my chamber?"

"They didn't search anything." He held up a letter with a big, broken red seal hanging from it. A very official-looking letter. "They brought this."

"What does it say?" Arabel breathed.

Leaning against the doorpost as though he couldn't quite hold himself up, Matthew cleared his throat and read. "'I thought fit to send this trumpet to you, to let you know that, if you please to walk away with your family and staff, and deliver your estate to such as I shall send to receive it, you shall have liberty to take one day to gather and carry off your goods, and such other necessaries as you have. You have failed to pay the fine assessed by the Committee for Compounding; if you necessitate me to bend my cannon against you, you may expect what I doubt you will not be pleased with. I await your present answer, and rest your servant, O. Cromwell.'"

"Oh, my God." Arabel's big brown eyes had never looked wider. "Did you give the soldiers your answer?"

"I had to. They wouldn't leave without it."

"And what was your answer?" Chrystabel asked impatiently. "What did you say?"

"That we'll leave, of course. Tomorrow, as he ordered. What else could I say?" Matthew straightened up. Some color had returned to his face. "The fine is a third of the value of this estate. I don't have that much money—Father spent all our savings on the war."

"The heartless bastards!" Chrystabel would be fined herself if the Dragoons heard her using that kind of language, but right now she didn't care. "How dare they!"

Matthew shrugged. "Our family dared to fight against them. Now they'll confiscate our estate for their own gain. They need funds to run the new government —if the king had won, he'd have robbed the other side just the same. We are but the spoils of war."

Matthew was a very levelheaded fellow, always good in a crisis. Unlike Chrystabel, who couldn't seem to think straight. "But what will we do? Where will we go?"

"Grosmont Castle." On his walk from the front door to her room, he'd obviously thought this through. "My seat. It's supported us ever since Father died. And it's the only place we *can* go, isn't it?" he added reasonably.

"We're to live in Wales?" Chrystabel shrieked, her volume not reasonable at all.

"My, that is far away," Arabel murmured.

"Yes, and what about all our friends?" Being a sociable sort, Chrystabel had many friends. "We won't make new ones—Wales is nothing but wilderness! And we don't even know their language! Their words have all those L's!"

"I'd wager there are no Dragoons there," Arabel

pointed out, looking on the bright side as always. "We won't need to worry about Cromwell coming after *that* drafty old castle."

"We can be thankful for that," Matthew agreed. "I imagine we should instruct the servants to begin packing our things."

Chrystabel shook her head, amazed that her brother could be so calm and practical. She remained silent a moment, struggling to resign herself to this dire fate.

Wales.

Wales!

She slipped a hand into her pocket and played with the silver pendant she kept there, which always made her feel better. Father had given it to her right before he left to go fight in the war, when she'd been inconsolable. It was a family heirloom, a rendering of the Grosmont crest with its lion, passed down the generations from father to son…and now to Chrystabel. Tradition said the lion pendant ought to be Matthew's, but Chrystabel only paid heed to traditions that suited her. And losing her dearest keepsake of the man she'd loved most in all the world would not suit her one bit.

Her heart constricted at the thought of everything else she was about to lose. Her ancient tester bed, where she'd spent most every night of her nineteen years. The harpsichord her mother used to play when they had company to supper. The little rose garden her father had planted for her…

"I'm taking my roses," she said suddenly, surprising even herself.

Matthew's dark brows knitted together. "What?"

"I'm taking my roses. I need them for essential oils to make perfume, and I haven't any idea whether there will be roses in Wales at all, let alone *my* roses."

Arabel shook her head. "They're *planted*, Chrystabel. You cannot take roses."

"What did Cromwell say?" Chrystabel marched over to snatch the letter from Matthew's hand and quote from it. "'You shall have liberty to take one day to gather and carry off your goods, and such other necessaries as you have.'" She looked up. "I'm a perfumer. I consider my roses necessary."

"You cannot take them," Arabel repeated. "There's no point. They'll die."

"It's winter. They're dormant." Chrystabel hoped that meant they wouldn't die.

"You cannot take them," Arabel insisted.

"You think not?" The look Chrystabel sent her sister was a challenge. "Watch me."

AVAILABLE NOW!
Learn more about *A Secret Christmas* at
www.LaurenRoyal.com

Read on for an excerpt from

Tempt Me
at Midnight

Book 1 of
Chase Family Series: The Regency
by Lauren Royal

Lady Alexandra Chase has always done what was expected of her. But when the man she's loved since her girlhood returns from a long spell abroad, she quite suddenly finds herself hoping the fine lord her brother has picked for her *won't* propose.

Cainewood Castle, the South of England
Summer 1808

IT WAS ALMOST like touching him.

Lady Alexandra Chase usually sketched a profile in just a few minutes, but she took her time today, lingering over the experience in the darkened room. Standing on one side of a large, framed pane of glass while Tristan sat sideways on the other, she traced his shadow cast by the glow of a candle. Her pencil followed his strong chin, his long, straight nose, the wide slope of his forehead, capturing his image on the sheet of paper she'd tacked to her side of the glass. Noticing a stray lock that tumbled down his brow, she hesitated, wanting to make certain she caught it just right.

Someone walked by the open door, causing Tris's shadow to flicker as the candle wavered. "Are you finished yet?" he asked from behind the glass panel.

"Hold still," she admonished, resisting the urge to peek around at him. "Artistry requires patience."

"This is a profile, not oil on canvas."

True, and she often wished she had the talent to paint, like her youngest sister, Corinna. But the fact that she was missing something Corinna had—that elusive, innate ability to see things others missed and convey them in color, light, and shade—didn't keep her from taking pride in her own hobby.

Alexandra made excellent profile portraits.

She'd been asking Tris to sit for her for years, but he'd never seemed to find time before. "You promised you'd sit still," she reminded him, knowing better than to read malice into his comment. "Just this once before you leave."

"I'm sitting," he said, and although his profile remained immobile, she could hear the laughter in his voice.

She loved that evidence of his control, just like she loved everything about Tris Nesbitt.

She'd been eight when they first met. Her favorite brother, Griffin, had brought him home between terms at school. In the many years since, as he and Griffin completed Eton and then Oxford, Tris had visited often, claiming to prefer his friend's large family to the quiet home he shared with his father.

Alexandra couldn't remember when she'd fallen in love, but she felt like she'd loved Tris forever.

Of course, nothing would ever come of it. Now, at fifteen, she was practical enough to accept that her father, the formidable Marquess of Cainewood, would never allow her to marry plain Mr. Tristan Nesbitt.

But that didn't stop her from wishing she could. It didn't stop her stomach from tingling when she heard his low voice, didn't stop her heart from skipping when she felt herself caught in his intense, silver-gray gaze.

Not that he directed his gaze her way often. It wasn't that he was unfriendly, but, after all, as far as he was concerned she was little more than Griffin's pesky younger sister.

Knowing Tris couldn't see her now, she skimmed her fingertips over his shadow, wishing she were touching *him* instead. She'd never touched him, not in real life. Such intimacy simply didn't occur between young ladies and men. Most especially between a marquess's daughter and an untitled man's son.

The drawing room's draperies were shut, and the resulting dimness seemed to afford them an odd closeness alone in the room. She traced the flow of his cravat illuminated through the glass onto her paper. "Where are you going again?" she asked, although she knew.

"Jamaica. My uncle wishes me to look after his interests. He owns a plantation there; I'm to learn how it's run."

He sounded sad. During this visit he'd seemed sad quite a bit. "Is that what you wish to do with your life?"

"He doesn't mean for me to stay there permanently. Only to acquaint myself with the operation so I can make intelligent decisions from afar."

"But do you wish to become his man of business? Do you want to manage his properties? Or would you rather do something else?"

He shrugged, his profile tilting, then settling back into the lines she'd so carefully drawn. "He financed my entire education. Have I a choice?"

"I suppose not." Her choices were limited, too. "How long will you be gone?"

"A year at the least, probably two, perhaps three."

Everything was changing. Griffin would leave soon as well—their father had bought him a commission in the cavalry. Although Griffin and Tris had spent much of the past few years at school and university, these new developments seemed different. They'd be across oceans. It wasn't that Alexandra would be alone—she'd still have her parents and her grandmother, her oldest brother and her two younger sisters—but she was already feeling the loss.

"Two or three years," she echoed, knowing Griffin would likely be gone even longer. "That seems a lifetime."

Tris's image shimmied as he laughed out loud. "I expect it might, to one as young as you."

He wasn't that much older, only one-and-twenty. But she supposed he'd seen a lot in the extra six years he had on her. Young men left home as adolescents to pursue their educations. They spent time hunting at country houses and carousing about London.

While she didn't exactly chafe at her own more restrictive life, she was counting the years and months until she'd turn eighteen and have her first season. She'd spent hour upon hour imagining the balls, the parties, and all the eligible young lords. One of those titled men would be her entrée to a new life as a society wife. A more exciting life, she hoped. And she would love her husband, she was certain, although right now she could hardly imagine loving any man besides Tris.

He'd never indicated any interest in her, but of course he wouldn't. As well as she, Tris knew his place. But that didn't stop her from wishing she knew whether he cared.

Just whether or not he cared.

"Will you bring me something from Jamaica?" she asked, startling herself with her boldness.

"Like what?" She heard astonishment in his voice. "A pineapple or some sugarcane?"

It was her turn to laugh. "Anything. Surprise me."

"All right, then. I will." He fell silent a moment, as though trying to commit the promise to memory. "Are you finished yet?"

"For now." She set down her pencil and walked to the windows, drew back the draperies, and blinked. The room's familiar blue-and-coral color scheme suddenly seemed too bright.

She turned toward him, reconciling his face with the profile she'd just sketched. From the boy she'd met years ago, he'd grown into a handsome, masculine man —one might even say he looked arresting. But she wouldn't describe him as pretty. His jaw was too strong, his mouth too wide, his brows too heavy and straight. As she watched, he raked a hand through his hair— tousled, streaky dark blond hair that always seemed just a bit too long.

Her fingers itched to run through it, to sweep the stray lock from his forehead.

"It will take me a while to complete the portrait," she told him as she walked back to where he sat beside the glass, "but I'll have it ready for you before you leave."

"Keep it for me."

She blew out the candle, leaning close enough to catch a whiff of his scent, smelling soap and starch and something uniquely Tris. "Don't you want it?"

He rose from the chair, smiling down at her from his greater height. "I'll probably lose it if I take it with me."

"Very well, then." She'd been hoping he'd say she should keep it to remember him by. But as always, Tris was the perfect gentleman. If he did harbor any affection for her, he wouldn't betray so with such a remark. "I wish you a safe journey, Mr. Nesbitt."

She'd called him Tristan—or Tris—for years now, but suddenly that seemed too informal.

His gray gaze remained steady. "Thank you, Lady Alexandra. I wish you a happy life."

A happy life. She could be married by the time he returned, she realized with a shock. In fact, if he were gone three years, she very likely would be.

Her heart sank at the thought.

But at least she'd have his profile. When she was finished, it would be black on white in an elegant oval frame, a perfect likeness of his face. And she'd almost touched him while making it.

As he walked from the room, she peeled the paper off the glass and hugged it to her chest.

AVAILABLE NOW!
Learn more about *Tempt Me at Midnight* at
www.LaurenRoyal.com

ENTER FOR A CHANCE TO WIN

a sterling silver replica of the pendant and earrings
that Aidan gives Amy in this book!*

Visit the Contest page on Lauren's website
at www.LaurenRoyal.com
and answer a question to be
entered in the monthly drawing.

No purchase necessary. See complete rules on the site.

*Please note: Depending on when you enter, the prize may be another piece of
jewelry associated with one of Lauren's books. The author reserves the right to
discontinue this promotion at any time.

ABOUT LAUREN ROYAL

 LAUREN ROYAL is a *New York Times* and *USA Today* bestselling author. Her "truly enchanting" novels have earned raves from reviewers including *Publishers Weekly*, who calls her "an impressive talent."

Lauren lives in Southern California with her family and their constantly shedding cat. When she's not busy writing, she enjoys singing along (off-key) to *Hamilton*, dancing (badly), and (wasting time) watching HGTV.

ACKNOWLEDGMENTS

My heartfelt thanks:

To my daughter, Devon, for her brilliant editing skills.

To my BFF and fellow author Glynnis Campbell, for helping me plot this story over brunch (although it was so long ago that she probably doesn't remember).

To my whole family, for the many (many!) discussions in the jacuzzi needed to refine the plot.

To everyone involved in making and bottling Trader Joe's Porto Morgado tawny port, for facilitating all of those discussions.

To my husband, Jack, for driving me all over the UK to find and explore all the homes I use in my books.

To one of my very favorite authors, Robert A. Heinlein, because I stole Cas and Pol's names from him, which makes him deserving of a mention even though he has left us and won't see this.

To all the honorary Chase cousins in my Chase Family Readers Group, for their enthusiastic support.

And to all of my readers, especially those of you who kept asking what happened to the Chase family after their original books ended.

Thank you, one and all!

CONTACT INFORMATION

Website

www.LaurenRoyal.com

Email

Lauren@LaurenRoyal.com

Newsletter

littl.ink/LaurensNews

Facebook Group

facebook.com/groups/ChaseFamilyReaders

Facebook Page

facebook.com/LaurenRoyal

Twitter

twitter.com/readLaurenRoyal

Instagram

instagram.com/readLaurenRoyal

www.ingramcontent.com/pod-product-compliance
Lightning Source LLC
Chambersburg PA
CBHW020405110726
47899CB00006B/1870